NO DARKNESS FOR LOVE

For lovely young Atalanta Lynton, the proposed marriage to her cousin William, Viscount Cottesford, seemed an answer to her prayers—until she found herself deeply in love with Paul Beaulieu, a handsome young painter. Atalanta is forced to choose between happiness and wealth in this passionate love story that vividly contrasts the glittering world of Paris with the colorful artist's life of Montmartre.

An enthralling bestseller
by the world's best loved writer
of romantic fiction
BARBARA CARTLAND

No Darkness for Love

Barbara Cartland

NO DARKNESS FOR LOVE
A Bantam Book / published January 1974

Bantam Books are published by Bantam Books, Inc. Its trade-
mark, consisting of the words "Bantam Books" and the por-
trayal of a bantam, is registered in the United States Patent
Office and in other countries. Marca Registrada. Bantam
Books, Inc., 666 Fifth Avenue, New York, New York 10019.

PRINTED IN THE UNITED STATES OF AMERICA

Author's Note

VALLON does not exist, but the description of the Impressionists and their lives are factual.

Le Chat Noir with its fantastic furnishings actually existed and its proprietor, Rodolphe Sarles, did much to popularise Montmartre. Renoir's model, Marie-Clementine Valadon, changed her Christian name to Suzanne and became a famous artist. She was the mother of the genius, Maurice Utrillo.

Spring by Claude Monet is in the National Galerie Berlin-Dahlem. *Le Moulin de la Galette* by Auguste Renoir, *Landscape at Chaponval* by Camille Pissarro, and many other pictures by the Impressionists which belong to the Louvre are on permanent exhibition in the Musée de Jeu de Pomme, Paris.

In 1803, Princess Pauline Borghese, sister of Napoleon Bonaparte, bought the present British Embassy in the Faubourg St. Honoré from the Duc de Chamort. The Duke of Wellington purchased the building for the

Princess in 1814. It was the first British Embassy ever owned by the British Government.

The cost of candles was a constant worry. Gas lighting was not installed until 1852, electricity in 1896; but an incoming Ambassador is still received with candles.

Chapter One

WALKING through the park under the shade of the great oak trees, where the daffodils were as golden as the Spring sunshine, Atalanta hummed a little tune to herself.

It was an inexpressible joy to think that, having got away early from the Castle, there was no reason for her to hurry home.

She could linger in the woods which were the shortest cut to the village, and where she had spent so much of her time when she was free from the innumerable tasks which engaged her at the Vicarage.

When she was a child, she had told herself stories in which the pine woods held fierce dragons from which she was rescued by a handsome Knight.

Even today, when she moved softly under the dark branches of the trees and felt the green moss springing under the lightness of her feet, she had the strange feeling that the tales which had filled her dreams for so many years would still come true!

1

Swinging her cotton sunbonnet by its strings, Atalanta was so intent on her own thoughts that she had nearly reached the edge of the wood before she looked up and saw, white between the trunks of two tall trees, the square of an artist's canvas.

In an instant, her happiness ebbed away. Mr. Oliver Whithorn was painting another picture of the Castle!

This meant he was in financial difficulties once again and would sell it to her soft-hearted Father, simply because no one else would be foolish enough to take it off his hands.

"There goes my new dress!" Atalanta thought despairingly.

Last time, it had been a winter coat of which Mr. Whithorn, with his excruciatingly badly painted picture, had deprived her.

There were by now no less than half a dozen of his canvases stacked in the attic, and Atalanta was convinced they were quite useless except for firewood.

She thought of turning aside and approaching the wood from another direction, but she realised that Mr. Whithorn must have seen her crossing the park and to avoid him deliberately would appear gratuitously ill-mannered.

Moving a little slower, now with no smile on her lips, Atalanta walked towards the easel set up in an all-too-familiar spot. Mr. Whithorn never chose any other viewpoint from which to execute his daubs of Combe Castle.

"Good afternoon, Mr. Whithorn. I see you are starting another masterpiece," Atalanta said, trying to keep the note of sarcasm out of her voice.

To her astonishment the man who rose from behind the canvas was not short, grey-haired, and ageing, but tall, dark, and bearing no resemblance whatsoever to the local artist.

"I regret, *Mademoiselle*," the Stranger said in a deep voice, "that I am not Mr. Oliver Whithorn."

"Oh, I am glad!" Atalanta exclaimed impetuously before she could prevent herself, then felt the colour come into her cheeks as she saw the twinkle in the Stranger's dark eyes.

His English had been perfect, but there was just a faint suspicion of an accent, and his addressing her as *Mademoiselle* made his identity clear.

"You are French!" she exclaimed, forgetting as usual that Mama had told her over and over again not to be too talkative or familiar with strangers.

"I thought as I saw you come across the park," the Stranger replied, "that you must be a small Goddess. You seemed to be part of the sunshine."

Two irresistible dimples appeared in Atalanta's cheeks.

"Alas! I am not a Goddess," she answered. "My name is Atalanta."

"The swift-footed huntress who could spring so lightly from crest to crest of a wave that she did not wet her feet!"

"I see, Sir, you have a knowledge of the Greek legend." Atalanta smiled. "That is unusual. Most people cannot understand why I have such an outlandish name."

"A very beautiful one and—very appropriate," the newcomer said quietly.

Again Atalanta felt the colour rising in her cheeks. She had not believed that any man could look at her with quite such a bold expression on his dark eyes, or indeed that she would find someone so unusual in the woods.

In fact, she told herself, she had never seen anyone like this strange man.

He was not so very young—she guessed him to be about twenty-eight or perhaps a little older—but he seemed taller and more broad-shouldered than she had expected a Frenchman to be.

His dark hair was swept back from a square forehead and his clear-cut features were decidedly handsome, even if he had an unusual appearance by English standards.

3

He wore, she noticed, a green-velvet coat such as might have been expected from an artist, and though his collar was of fashionable height his tie was distinctly floppy.

He stood there, looking at her, and because the expression in his eyes made her feel shy, she said quickly as if to draw away attention from herself: "You speak very good English, Sir."

"My Grandmother was English," he answered. "*Et vous, Mademoiselle, parlez vous français?*"

Atalanta smiled.

"*Oui, Monsieur,*" she replied in French, "my Grandmother was French!"

"*C'est extraordinaire!*" the stranger exclaimed. "And may I add I also had an English Nurse."

"So did I," Atalanta said, "but I assure you she never did hold with 'them foreigners across the water.'"

The Stranger threw back his head and laughed.

"My Nurse always said, 'You can't help where you were born, poor child, but I'll make you into a gentleman if I die in the attempt.'"

They were both laughing, and then, as if Atalanta suddenly realised the irresponsible manner in which she was behaving, she said demurely: "I hope, Sir, you enjoy painting the Castle. It is very beautiful."

As she spoke, she turned away to follow the path through the wood.

"Wait! Wait!" the Stranger said quickly. "Please do not leave me! There is so much I want to know."

"I think . . . I should . . . go." Atalanta faltered.

She was intensely curious about this Stranger, but at the same time she knew her Mother would not approve.

It was one thing to pass the time of day—everyone did that in the country—but it was quite different to linger, chatting and laughing with a man to whom she had not even been introduced.

As if he read her thoughts, the artist said almost pleadingly: "Do you not realise that our Nurses, had they been with us, would undoubtedly have talked to each other? We would have been introduced from our perambulators."

He hesitated, then added: "*Alors!* I should no longer have been in my perambulator, would I? Yet, if we had met in the Bois or in Hyde Park, I am sure I should have been told to amuse you while our Nurses gossiped about their employers."

He saw the smile on Atalanta's face and added: "May I therefore present myself? Paul Beaulieu, *Mademoiselle,* at your service."

Atalanta dropped him a small curtsey.

"Atalanta Lynton."

"And you are the Princess who lives in that magnificent Castle?" he asked.

Atalanta shook her head.

"No indeed," she said, "I am only the poor relation."

He raised his dark eyebrows.

"Poor relation?" he questioned in puzzled tones.

"The Princess, as you have called her, is Lady Clementine Combe," Atalanta explained. "She lives in the Castle and is spoken of as the 'most beautiful girl in England.'"

"And you?" Paul Beaulieu enquired.

"I am her cousin and live in Little Combe. My father is the Vicar. He is also a Greek scholar, hence my name."

Again the dimples appeared in Atalanta's cheeks: "My twin sisters were christened Chryseis and Hebe and resent it very much! They would so much rather have been called Emily and Edith or something quite unexceptional."

"And you?" Paul Beaulieu enquired.

"I am content to be Atalanta, but then I enjoy reading Greek."

"For the first time in my life," Paul Beaulieu said, "I do not regret the long hours I spent struggling with that very complicated alphabet and being reprimanded by my tutor for not pronouncing the poetry of Homer in the correct manner."

5

"And yet later one comes to realise it is fascinating," Atalanta said.

"Fascinating indeed!" Paul Beaulieu agreed.

He was looking at Atalanta as he spoke, seeing her tiny pointed face with its huge grey-blue eyes which seemed to reflect their owner's feelings as clearly as the clouds crossing a sunlit sky.

And above the oval forehead there was that very pale golden hair which had made him believe, as he had seen her walking through the park, that she was the very embodiment of Spring.

Her well-washed cotton dress was unfashionable, and it clung, because she had almost grown out of it, to the budding maturity of her small breasts.

There was a grace about her which made him think once again that she was aptly named.

"I want to paint you," he said suddenly. "It is not often an artist gets a chance to portray the heroine of a Greek legend who looks like a Goddess. Please stay! Already I have the idea of how I wish you to pose."

"But surely you were painting the Castle," Atalanta objected. "May I see what you have done?"

"I should be honoured," Paul Beaulieu answered, standing aside so that she could draw near to his easel.

Atalanta had seen many pictures of the Castle. All down the centuries it had attracted famous artists and there were many versions of it in the Picture Gallery.

There were conversation pieces depicting the various Earls of Winchcombe with their families with the Castle in the background or, as Turner and Constable had painted it, silhouetted against the setting sun.

Originally Norman, on one side the great grey tower stood sentinel over the countryside.

The main building had been added to generation after generation until, now one of the largest private houses in England, it was a symbol of the wealth, importance, and prestige of the Winchcombe family.

Seen from close up, as Atalanta knew only too well, it was rather overpowering and awe-inspiring. But from

6

the distance, it had an almost fairylike quality and this Paul Beaulieu had captured in his picture, which was unlike any she had ever seen before.

She stood looking wide-eyed at the brilliance of the colours, at the foreground in which the daffodils, vividly gold and compelling, seemed to lead the eye toward the mystical majesty of the tower etched against the blue and white of the sky.

The way Paul Beaulieu painted it was different. No black, a radiance of colour, every stone seeming through the light falling on it to have a vibration and a movement.

It was different from anything she had seen. Then suddenly she knew!

"You are an Impressionist!" she exclaimed.

Paul Beaulieu, who had been watching her face, said quietly: "And what do you know about Impressionists?"

"I have read about them," Atalanta answered, "and Papa has told me how they have been abused and scorned in Paris."

"And you—what do you think of my picture?" Paul Beaulieu asked.

"It is very beautiful," Atalanta said softly.

"Do you mean that?" he asked.

"Of course I mean it," she replied. "I would not lie, even to flatter you, about something so important."

"I never thought," he said slowly, "that an English woman would appreciate what a few revolutionary men are trying to convey on canvas."

"Papa has told me," Atalanta said, "that the Salon and most Art dealers in France believe that art does not consist of painting what one sees, but what is conventional to see. You, I think, are painting what is in your heart."

"You are very perceptive," Paul Beaulieu said, "and now let me paint you."

"I ought not to stay," Atalanta replied, hesitating. "They are expecting me at home."

"Please—it would be a great kindness! I cannot tell

7

you how much I want to capture your little face on canvas. I have never before seen anyone so lovely."

She blushed at the compliment. Then she told herself
he was only trying to cajole her into sitting for him.
Perhaps he found it difficult to pay a model.

Had not Papa said that the Impressionists starved
themselves for their pictures? Paul Beaulieu might have
to go without meals so that he could purchase his
paints.

If so, he certainly would not be able to afford the fees
of those who made their living by modeling.

"I cannot stay for long," Atalanta said.

She remembered guiltily the chickens which had to
be fed, the horses that were waiting for her to give them
their hay, and the innumerable other tasks she was
neglecting at home.

And yet she told her conscience she had been early
leaving the Castle.

Cicely had been told she was to have her rest an hour
earlier because her brother William was expected home
from Paris that evening.

The Viscount Cottesford was in the Diplomatic Service and was usually abroad. But now the whole household was in a state of excitement because a telegram
had announced his arrival.

"There must be at least half an hour left," Atalanta
thought, "before Mama will be expecting me."

Paul Beaulieu was already picking up his easel and
carrying it with a heavy leather bag further into the
wood.

"Where are you going to paint me?" Atalanta asked.

"Against the fir trees," he answered. "I want you to
look as if you have come from the sunshine into the
cool of the pines."

He found a place where there was a felled tree
covered with moss on which Atalanta could sit.

A shaft of sunlight slanting through the thick branches
just touched the pale gold of her head, haloing her curls

and lighting up her eyes so that they seemed to be no longer blue, but to reflect the green of the trees.

Paul Beaulieu set up his easel a little way from Atalanta and then he walked towards her, narrowing his eyes as if to get her into perspective, noting the way that she sat naturally on the tree trunk with a grace which could never be taught.

She had linked her fingers together in her lap and now she looked up at him, her eyes enquiring and curious, at the same time a little shy.

It was as if she suddenly realised how big he was, how different in his dark handsome way from any man she had ever met before!

"*Voila!* That is perfect," he said gently.

He went back to his easel, moving it just slightly so that in the distance to the right of Atalanta there was just a glimpse of the Castle, brilliant in the afternoon sunshine.

He drew a new canvas from the leather bag and picked up his palette.

"Talk," he said. "I do not want you stiff or self-conscious. Tell me about yourself. Why do you say you are the poor relation?"

"My Uncle Lionel—the present Earl of Winchcombe —is Mama's half brother," Atalanta answered. "He is a rather frightening person, but very important, very rich. Papa and Mama fell in love with each other and, after long years of waiting, they were allowed to get married. But we are very poor!"

"Do you mind being poor?" Paul Beaulieu asked.

"Not really," Atalanta answered. "I have almost everything I want except new dresses. But my brother, Bernard, minds as he wants to go into the Army, which Papa cannot afford, and the twins mind terribly."

"It would surely be very easy for you to be rich," Paul Beaulieu remarked.

"Me? How could I?" Atalanta enquired in surprise.

"You could marry a rich man!"

9

"Nobody asked me, Sir, she said!" Atalanta laughed. "And I have no wish to marry for money."

"You would rather marry for love?" Paul Beaulieu questioned.

"But of course." Atalanta's voice was very positive.

"And supposing you never fall in love?"

"Then I must die an old maid!" Atalanta replied.

"Never! Never! It would be a crime against nature!" Paul Beaulieu cried. "But let me predict your future. One day you will fall in love, and you will love passionately, deeply, and irrevocably!"

"How do you know that?" Atalanta asked almost in a whisper.

"I can tell it by your mouth and by your eyes," he answered. "Women with lips like yours are givers and you will give to the man you love your heart, your body, and your soul."

There was a note in his voice which made Atalanta draw in her breath and her eyes dropped as the blood rose in her cheeks.

"You should not be painting me, but my cousin Clementine," she said quickly in an effort to change the subject. "She is lovely, really lovely!"

"Is it possible she could be more beautiful than you?" Paul Beaulieu asked.

He spoke in such a matter-of-fact tone that Atalanta was not embarrassed.

"You are teasing me," she replied. "I am not beautiful. But Clementine has perfect features, classical like a statue, and her hair is the colour of ripened corn and her eyes are really blue. Pale blue like a thrush's egg."

"You certainly admire her!" Paul Beaulieu remarked. "Are you also fond of her?"

There was a little hesitation before Atalanta said: "She is older than I am, and as she moves in the very best society, we have very little in common. It is Cicely whom I love."

"And who is Cicely?" Paul Beaulieu enquired.

"She is Clementine's sister—Lady Cicely Combe. She

10

had a riding accident a year ago and has to lie flat on her back. The doctors hope she will be able to walk again, but there is always the fear that she may not be able to do so."

Atalanta gave a little sigh.

"Poor Cicely! It is very hard for her! You can imagine what it must be like at seventeen to have nothing to do but lie flat and to think of other people riding and dancing and doing all the things that one longs to do one's self."

"And so you go and talk to her?"

"We gossip! Cicely likes to collect information about everybody inside and outside the Castle," Atalanta said. "And we read together. Cicely has a good brain. I think really she ought to have been a boy. She enjoys Latin, I am teaching her Greek, and we read Molière, Balzac, and Goethe together, and of course the novels written by Dickens and the Brontes."

"I am glad of the last two authors," Paul Beaulieu said, smiling. "I was beginning to be afraid that you and Cicely were blue stockings!"

"Would that shock you?" Atalanta said. "Mama always says that men hate clever women. She tells me that when I go to parties I must not show off my knowledge, but appear quiet, feminine, and admiring to the man I am with."

"And do you do that?" Paul Beaulieu enquired.

Atalanta smiled, and he saw her irrepressible dimples.

"I very seldom go to parties," she answered, "but when I do I usually forget to be quiet and admiring. Perhaps that is why I have so few beaux."

"Are all the men in this part of England blind?" Paul Beaulieu asked.

"No, they are too busy looking at Clementine." Atalanta smiled. "Just as you would be if you saw her. Then you would not want to paint me—you would want to paint her."

"I very much doubt it," Paul Beaulieu said. "And may

11

I say, little Goddess, that I am very content and very grateful that you have been kind enough to sit for me."

"Perhaps an Impressionist would not do Clementine justice," Atalanta remarked seriously as if she was following her own train of thought.

"I am sure she needs a proper Academician," Paul Beaulieu said. "He would paint her in white satin with a string of pearls and a bunch of pink roses in her hand. The golden hair and the blue eyes would, of course, be best against a draped curtain of blue velvet."

There was no mistaking the sarcasm in his voice and Atalanta laughed.

"That is exactly how she has been painted! Not once, but twice. The pictures are hanging in the Castle. I would so much like to show them to you!"

"I would like to see them," Paul Beaulieu said. "They would, I am sure, be an excellent example to a young artist of how to get himself hung in the Royal Academy and make his fortune."

"Do you not want to make a fortune?" Atalanta enquired.

"Not particularly," he answered, "but I would like more people to understand the message the Impressionists are trying to convey. The Master under whom I have studied had a picture accepted by the Salon last year, but he is so impoverished that he has pawned almost everything he owns."

"How tragic!" Atalanta exclaimed. "What is your Master's name?"

"His name is Claude Monet," Paul Beaulieu answered.

"Oh, but I have seen one of his pictures!" Atalanta cried. "I mean I have seen a photograph of it. It was sent to Papa by one of his friends who was visiting Paris. It was called *Spring Landscape*."

"Monet painted that in 1874, six years ago," Paul Beaulieu said. "You liked it?"

"I thought it very, very beautiful," Atalanta answered. "Now I can understand how, with what seems only a few strokes of the brush, you can make the Castle seem so mysterious and make me feel that the daffodils in the park are alive."

Paul Beaulieu put down his palette and stared at her.

"You know," he said, "you are a very remarkable person, besides being utterly and completely lovely."

His words seemed to startle Atalanta or perhaps it was the way he spoke in his deep voice. She clasped her fingers a little tighter and stared at him, her eyes very large.

Then it seemed to her that something passed between her and the man looking at her—something she did not understand, yet which seemed to her to comprise the magic of his picture and the picture she had seen by Claude Monet.

There was something compelling and fascinating about it and, at the same time, a little frightening.

Without really meaning to do so, she rose to her feet.

"I must . . . go," she said. "I am sure . . . it is getting late . . . Mama will be . . . expecting me."

"Will you come tomorrow?"

"I do not . . . know," Atalanta answered. "It may be difficult . . . and I shall not have so much . . . time."

"Please make time," Paul Beaulieu pleaded. "That is what my Nurse always used to say. 'You must make time'—and somehow I always managed to do so."

He drew nearer to her as he spoke and now she found herself looking up at him.

He was so much taller than she was and she had the extraordinary feeling that, though they had just met, she had known him before. He did not seem a stranger; there was a familiarity about him as if he had been in her life a long time.

"Please come!" he said softly, his eyes searching her face. "I cannot lose you now. Perhaps this picture of you will bring me fame and fortune. If it was never finished, you would have it on your conscience forever that you had denied me those two rewards."

13

He spoke with sincerity and yet there was a twinkle in his eyes.

"You are flattering me into believing that I am important," Atalanta replied. "Have I not told you that I am just the poor relation?"

"On the contrary, you are undoubtedly a Goddess sent to bemuse poor mortals like myself. Will you bring me a gift from Olympus?"

She smiled up at him.

"I will do my best," she answered, "and I will come tomorrow, though I may not be able to stay long."

"I shall be waiting," he said, and she had the feeling that the words were important.

He put out his hand as he spoke and took hers. She thought they would shake hands, but instead he raised it to his lips, and she felt the pressure of his mouth against her skin.

It was not what she had expected and her heart gave a frightened leap.

Then she had turned and hurried away from him through the woods, twisting her way through the thick trunks of the trees until finally she vanished into the shadows and he could see her no longer.

He stood for some minutes staring after her, and then he sat down again in front of his easel and began to paint feverishly, with a fierce concentration, as if every stroke was etched strongly in his mind before he put it on the canvas.

Atalanta ran from the wood onto the narrow dusty road which led into the village.

The clock on the small grey-stone Church told her it was nearly a quarter to five o'clock and she knew that her Mother was sure to ask why she had stayed so late at the Castle.

Atalanta seldom told a lie, but she was determined if possible not to reveal the reason for her tardiness or to mention the presence of a stranger in the woods.

There would not only be innumerable questions as to who he was and what he was doing, but she was also

14

quite certain that the twins would not miss the opportunity of making the acquaintance of a foreigner.

At fifteen they were both incurably romantic and what was more they were determined, as Atalanta had never been, to escape from the confinement of village life and the poverty of the Vicarage.

As she thought of the twins, Atalanta gave a little sigh as she slipped through the gate into the Vicarage. Instead of going toward the house, she went to feed the chickens in the orchard behind the stables.

"If only one of Papa's books could be a success!" she said to herself.

It was a sentiment that had been expressed over and over again by Lady Evelyn Lynton.

She had braved her Father's wrath and the contempt of her half-brother when she had insisted on marrying not one of the important suitors who had paid court to her when she was first taken to London for the Season, but the third and impoverished son of Sir Perquine Lynton.

He was quite unacceptable to her parents as a future husband and Evelyn had been told so in no uncertain terms.

It had taken Donatus Lynton and Evelyn Combe five years to obtain permission to be husband and wife. It was only after Evelyn had turned down suitor after suitor and finally had refused the Duke of Loth that her Father had washed his hands of her.

"Very well—go to the devil in your own way!" he had said bluntly.

The only concession the Earl had made, when finally his daughter married the quiet, scholarly Donatus, was to offer them the living at Little Combe, which brought them in a yearly income of three hundred pounds.

It was certainly not the life to which Lady Evelyn had been accustomed, but being deeply in love with her unworldly husband she had asked for nothing except that they could be together.

It was when the children came that problems arose.

Bernard was so handsome and such a good sportsman, besides inheriting his father's brain, that she resented his not having decent horses to ride and being unable to dress as smartly as his friends.

Lady Evelyn watched Atalanta grow more and more attractive, knowing that if she were fashionably gowned she would outshine any of her counterparts.

Finally the twins, who were far more worldly than the rest of the family, clamoured incessantly for new clothes, for bigger ponies, for parties and social activities.

"If only one of Papa's books could be a success!" Lady Evelyn would murmur.

But she had no idea how disrespectful the twins were about the erudite volumes their Father produced every two years. The books commanded the respect and admiration of a few scholarly Dons, but were of no interest to the general public.

Unfortunately, as Atalanta knew only too well, the books occupied her Father's attention to the exclusion of all else. He was apt to forget a funeral, a christening, even a wedding.

The villagers, who were used to his absent-minded irregularities, would say to one of their children: "Hop up to th' Vicarage, Tommy, and remind the Reverend that th' body be coming along in a quarter o' th' hour. Help him into his surplice and don't ye dare leave his side until he be a standing by th' grave."

Atalanta, while feeding the chickens, remembered that her Father had a meeting with the Church Wardens at five o' clock.

She gave the horses several forkfuls of hay, picked up the new-laid eggs she had collected from the hens' nests, and hurried into the house. She put the eggs into the kitchen and then walked down the passage towards the Drawing Room.

Lady Evelyn was sitting on the sofa, sewing small bone buttons onto one of Hebe's blouses.

"Oh, there you are, Atalanta!" she exclaimed. "I was wondering what had happened to you."

"I have been feeding the chickens, Mama," Atalanta said truthfully, "and I was just coming to remind Papa he has a Church meeting at five o'clock."

"Heavens, I had forgotten!" Lady Evelyn exclaimed. "What a good thing you remembered. Go and get Papa ready, Atalanta, and do see he is wearing a tie and not those carpet slippers in which he went to the last meeting."

"I will see to it, Mama," Atalanta said.

Thankful to be asked no more questions about her lateness, she hurried to the Study.

She got her Father ready for the meeting, although he expostulated vigorously about being disturbed.

"Must I attend it, Atalanta?" he asked plaintively. "I have just reached a really interesting part in my sixth chapter. If I leave it now, I am certain to lose my train of thought."

"I am sorry, Papa, but you must go to the meeting," Atalanta said firmly. "You must discuss the repairs to the Church Tower and the accounts for this year from March 1879 to March 1880. Do not agree to everything that horrid Lady Boddington suggests. You know she only argues just to prove how important she is."

The Vicar put down his manuscript reluctantly.

"I was just writing about the Egyptian influence on early Greek civilisation," he said. "It is extremely interesting, Atalanta."

"You must read it to me, Papa," Atalanta said, "but not at this moment. Now you must attend the meeting."

"Very well," the Vicar said with a sigh, "but it does seem that I am always interrupted at the worst possible moment."

"I know, Papa, but it cannot be helped," Atalanta said sympathetically.

She was shepherding her Father from the room when she saw a basket covered with a white cloth on a side table.

17

"Papa!" she exclaimed. "Did not Henry Gorton call to-day with a message from his mother?"

"Henry—Gorton—yes, I think he did," the Vicar answered.

"But Papa you know you had to give him that special medicine that Mama had made for Mrs. Gorton. You must have forgotten, for it is still there on the table."

"Oh, dear, I am afraid it slipped my mind," the Vicar said, looking extremely guilty.

"Never mind, Papa, I will take it to Mrs. Gorton. She says that Mama's special herbs are the only thing which helps her pain. Now, go straight to the Vestry! Do not stop or think of anything else or you will be late. You promise me?"

"Of course! Of course!" the Vicar replied.

With a sigh, Atalanta picked up the basket containing the special herbal medicine that her Mother had spent several hours making for Mrs. Gorton.

It was so like her Father to forget it and Henry, aged ten, was a scatterbrained little boy who would not remember anything he had been asked to bring back.

It would not take her more than twenty minutes to walk to the Gortons' house, and then perhaps her Mother would not know that her Father had been forgetful once again.

Not that Lady Evelyn was ever cross with her beloved husband, but at the same time it distressed her to see him growing more and more indifferent to the needs of the villagers and more and more obsessed with his writing.

If only Papa's books earned more money, Atalanta thought, he would be able to have help with the Church services and Mama could afford a better type of servant.

She and her Mother trained the local village girls, but as soon as they learned the rudiments of housework or cooking, they knew they could go up to the Castle and earn more money, besides having the prestige of being in service to the Earl of Winchcombe.

Only her Mother, Atalanta thought, would be able to smile when the Housekeeper at the Castle said:

"The last two girls we had from you, M'Lady, were real treasures—hard workers and well up in their duties. I often say to Her Ladyship we ought to be real grateful for the Vicarage maids, that we ought."

But that was cold comfort for all the hours she and her Mother spent explaining to some nitwit how to lay a table, how to polish a grate, how to make a bed!

She picked up her sunbonnet automatically and, with the basket on her arm, let herself out of the back door of the Vicarage to set off across the fields to the Gortons' house.

Mrs. Gorton, a widow, was one of those helpless people who were always ailing, always complaining. She had enough money to be comfortable, but not enough to entertain in the way she would have liked, and to command attention she had to be continually ill.

Now she had got it into her head that the only thing that really helped her was Lady Evelyn's homemade herbs and medicine.

It meant a lot of extra work, as Atalanta knew only too well.

Her Mother had to give up precious time to pick, dry, and mix the herbs, which Atalanta often thought were not really necessary because what Mrs. Gorton really needed was another husband.

However, such a revolutionary and improper idea would not have been acceptable either to her mother or her father, so she kept it to herself. But as she trudged across the fields carrying the basket on her arm, she was not thinking of Mrs. Gorton, but of the strange young man she had met in the woods.

How good-looking he was, and how manly he appeared despite his velvet jacket and his flowing tie!

She had not expected a painter to seem so virile. She had always thought of them as rather effeminate, but then her experience of artists was very limited.

She had met one of the fashionable portrait painters

who had painted Clementine. He had been an affected vacillating creature, with a weak chin which he disguised with a pointed beard.

He had spoken in an almost falsetto voice, and while she knew he commanded large sums from his clients, she had not admired either his painting or the man himself.

Paul Beaulieu was very different. There was something determined, almost authoritative, about him, something which told Atalanta very clearly that he would succeed in anything he undertook.

Perhaps one day he would be acclaimed as a genius. Perhaps her portrait would bring him fame and fortune, and yet he had said that he was not particularly interested in a fortune. Was it fame he sought?

Atalanta found herself puzzling about him and that moment of magic which had made her run away.

It was wrong of him to look at her in just that manner, she told herself, and yet she had to admit that it had not annoyed her.

There was no doubt she had behaved in a very reprehensible manner. How would she ever explain to Mama that she had talked for nearly an hour to a stranger in the woods?

Then she knew that, whatever Mama might say if she heard of it, she would talk to Paul Beaulieu again tomorrow and sit while he painted her portrait. She could hardly wait for the hours to pass until she could see him again.

It did not take as long as Atalanta had expected to reach Mrs. Gorton's house.

Having handed over the medicine to the smartly dressed parlour maid who answered the door, Atalanta managed to slip away without having to see Mrs. Gorton.

She knew that once she entered the Drawing Room, she would have to listen to Mrs. Gorton's long list of imaginary ailments and also an even longer list of Henry's misdemeanours and mischievous pranks.

It was always the same: the wretched little boy had not enough to do and no companions, so he merely succeeded in irritating his mother, who tried to evoke sympathy from anyone who would listen to her tales of helplessness in bringing up her only child.

The sun was sinking in a blaze of glory as Atalanta wended her way back over the fields towards the Vicarage.

Intent on her own thoughts, she had entered the stableyard and was crossing the cobbles toward the house before she realised that a very smart Phaeton, drawn by two horses, was standing outside the front door.

There was a groom wearing a cockaded tophat and the Winchcombe livery with its crested buttons, and Atalanta wondered why someone from the Castle should be calling at this time of day.

If the Earl or Countess had sent a note to her Father or Mother, a groom would have carried it on horseback. Although the Earl might drive the Phaeton, the Countess would certainly have come in a closed carriage.

Atalanta wondered what could have happened, and why Uncle Lionel should want to see Mama.

She entered the house through the back door of the Vicarage and, catching a glimpse of herself in one of the mirrors decorating the passage, she stopped to tidy her hair.

Blown by the evening wind, she looked what her mother would call a "sad romp" and she knew that Clementine would never allow herself to get in such a state.

Atalanta wondered if she should go upstairs and change her dress. The walk over the fields had left the hem damp and the pollen from the wild flowers had marked it.

Then she gave her shoulders a little shrug. What did it matter? Whoever was in the Drawing Room would not have come to see her.

She would go in and say, "How do you do," because it

would be polite, but if, as she suspected, it was Uncle Lionel who was paying them a visit, he would not be interested in her or in her appearance.

Pushing her hair back from her forehead, Atalanta opened the door of the Dining Room and walked in.

To her surprise, both her Father and Mother were present and also a man who was not her Uncle and who for a moment she did not recognise.

Then she realised it was her cousin, William—Viscount Cottesford—whom she had not seen for over three years.

When William was at the Castle, he had never had any time for Cousin Atalanta, whom he had always found extremely tiresome as a small girl and ignored when she grew older.

"Atalanta!" Lady Evelyn exclaimed as her daughter appeared. "I was just wondering where you were."

She moved across the room as she spoke, looking exceedingly happy, her eyes shining, and it seemed to Atalanta's surprised gaze that years of worry and anxiety had suddenly dropped from her once-lovely face.

"Atalanta, my dear, dear child!" she said and kissed her daughter's cheek.

Astonished, Atalanta looked towards her Father, who was also smiling at her, and then towards her cousin.

She had always thought him stiff, stuck-up, and disagreeable, but she had learnt enough of male fashion from Bernard to realise that with his high collar and stylishly cut clothes, Cousin William was exceedingly smart.

He looked older, but then he must by now be at least thirty-eight and that, Atalanta thought, was really getting on in years.

She had always been a little afraid of Cousin William, and yet at this moment she had never seen him look more pleasant.

"What is it?" she asked. "What has happened?"

"Something very marvellous, darling," Lady Evelyn

replied, "something which I know will make you as happy as it has made Papa and me."

She paused and once again kissed her daughter's cheek.

"What can it be?" Atalanta enquired.

"Your Cousin William—dear William," Lady Evelyn replied, "has asked Papa for your hand in marriage."

Chapter Two

AFTERWARDS Atalanta could never remember what she had said, or if she had said anything at all.

She could only recall her Mother's excited voice and the moment when she realised William was looking at her untidy hair, his eyes glancing critically at her too-tight cotton dress with its damp hem.

He had always made her feel awkward and uncomfortable, and now she regretted that she had not gone upstairs first to change her dress before entering the Drawing Room. It was, however, only a momentary feeling of embarrassment.

Her Father put his arm around her and said: "What your mother and I want, Atalanta, is your happiness."

Then turning to William, he went on: "You will find Atalanta a very intelligent and unusual girl. She knows Greek almost as well as I do and Latin comes easily to her."

"What is more important," Lady Evelyn interposed, "Atalanta speaks perfect French and very good Italian.

She will find that very useful as the wife of a Diplomat."

Atalanta found she could not look at her cousin's face.

"They are enumerating my points as if I were a filly at a Horse Fair," she thought, and then was ashamed that she should have such ideas at such a moment.

"There is a great deal of planning to do," William said at length in a voice which seemed to Atalanta to be cold and distant, as if he found her parents' gushing enthusiasm distasteful.

"Of course," Lady Evelyn agreed, "but there is no hurry."

"Unfortunately there is," William answered. "My Mother will explain everything to you this evening. She is expecting you and Uncle Donatus to dinner and Atalanta of course."

"To dinner!" Lady Evelyn exclaimed in dismay with a glance at the clock on the mantelpiece.

"I will send a carriage for you at seven-thirty," William said and moved towards the door.

Lady Evelyn accompanied him, talking all the time in that high excited voice which Atalanta thought made her seem almost as young as the twins.

As they left the room, Atalanta turned to her Father, a look of enquiry in her eyes.

"You will be happy with your cousin," he said before she could speak. "He is extremely intelligent and has already made his mark in the Diplomatic Service."

"Yes, I know, Papa!"

Atalanta wanted to say a great deal more, but her Father turned away and she knew he was in a hurry to get back to his study. His thoughts were no longer with her, but in Ancient Greece.

She ran upstairs to find the twins waiting on the landing. They danced around her, hysterical with delight.

"We listened!" they cried. "We listened at the door! We thought it strange that Cousin William should call on Papa and Mama, so we listened! Oh, Atalanta, how wonderful! Think of all you can do for us, the clothes

25

you can give us, the parties we can go to with you as a chaperone!"

Atalanta, even if she had wanted to say something, would have found it impossible to make her voice heard.

"You will be a Viscountess until Uncle Lionel dies," Hebe said solemnly, "a Viscountess, think of it, Atalanta! And when you are a Countess you will live at the Castle, and Aunt Louise will have to move into the Dower House."

Atalanta was not paying attention. She was at her wardrobe, trying to find a dress to wear for dinner.

Clementine's old clothes were always sent down to the Vicarage eventually, but she had a habit of keeping them for three or four years until they were practically out of fashion.

Even if she was no longer wearing them, they still hung in her wardrobe.

It was on a par, Atalanta knew, with the careful cheese-paring that was characteristic of both her uncle and her aunt. The Earl might be extremely wealthy, but he disliked spending money on what he considered unessential things.

The wages at the Castle were not high. The pensioners received less than on neighbouring estates. The meals, when the family was alone, were by no means as elaborate as in other establishments of the Earl's contemporaries, and nearly every month there was a stormy scene over the size of the housekeeping bills.

Both the Countess and Clementine went to the best Court dressmakers in London for their gowns, but they bought comparatively few and these were made to last a very long time.

By the time the day gowns, the cloaks, the *toilettes de soir* reached the Vicarage, they were not only out of date but usually almost threadbare.

Fortunately Atalanta was shorter than her cousin. At least three inches had to be taken off every hem and that meant that the worn edge could be skillfully concealed by Lady Evelyn's or Atalanta's clever needle.

It was also a considerable satisfaction to realise that Clementine, elegant and beautiful though she was, was two inches bigger in the waist, and invariably the dress had to be taken in around the bust.

"I am sick of old clothes!" Atalanta had said to Lady Evelyn when the last trunkful of worn garments had arrived at the Vicarage.

"I know, darling," Lady Evelyn replied. "And you would think that your cousin might at least get her Lady's maid to clean them before they are sent to us."

It was seldom that Lady Evelyn criticised the manner in which she was treated by her half brother and his wife.

But Atalanta missed none of the snubs, the casual indifference, the manner in which, when they were entertained, the Countess invariably made the party from the Vicarage feel they were unimportant outsiders.

Now Atalanta looked at the gowns hanging in her wardrobe and realised that William would undoubtedly view them with the contempt they deserved.

Finally she drew out a dress of white gauze which had arrived sadly torn on one side, where Clementine must have caught it in the door of a carriage, but was otherwise less worn than many of the others.

She undressed, and washed quickly while the twins jumped around the room and chattered all the time about the grandeur that would be hers in the future.

"You will be asked to all the important balls in London," Chryseis said. "Perhaps you will even be invited to Windsor Castle. Think if you should actually meet the Queen!"

"I am much more concerned at the moment in not being late for dinner at the Castle," Atalanta replied. "Do be an angel, Chryseis, and find my evening slippers and, Hebe, see if you can do anything to my hair."

"You looked as if you had been through a haystack backwards when you went into the Drawing Room," Hebe said. "We wanted to warn you, but we did not get a chance. Papa had just come out to get something from the study to show Cousin William and we had to scuttle upstairs; otherwise he would have realised that we had been listening at the door!"

"I cannot think how you can be so ill-bred," Atalanta said disapprovingly, but even as she spoke she knew the twins were not listening to her.

"William is very smart," Chryseis said. "Did you see how well his coat was cut? Bernard would die of envy! His cravat had not a wrinkle in it anywhere!"

"Yes, he is smart," Hebe agreed as her clever fingers pinned into place the long fair curls at the back of Atalanta's head. "But he is old! He will be thirty-nine next birthday. That makes him twenty years older than you."

Atalanta had not answered, but at the same time Hebe's words seemed to throb in her head as she drove in the Earl's comfortable and well-cushioned carriage toward the Castle.

"Twenty years older!"

She sat on the small seat opposite her Father and Mother, and she found herself thinking that when she married William she would be able to drive in a carriage just as grand as this and sit facing the horses.

"You will be able to do so much for the girls," Lady Evelyn was saying, "and, you know, although your Uncle Lionel said he would pay Bernard's fees at Oxford, he would not give him an allowance or any spending money at all. Bernard feels it dreadfully that he is so much poorer than all the other men in his College."

"It is no use anticipating the future, Evelyn," the Reverend Donatus said quietly. "We have no idea yet what the Marriage Settlement will be, or if William will allow Atalanta enough money for her to be able to be generous to her family."

"But Donatus, my dearest, you must insist that he provides in a correct manner for Atalanta! You know as well as I do that a Marriage Settlement is of the utmost importance."

"I will do my best, my love," the Vicar answered vaguely. "But as I can bring nothing into the Settlement, I am not really in a position to argue as to how generous the Bridegroom or his father should be."

Lady Evelyn was about to say more and then Atalanta saw her press her lips together.

She knew her Mother was feeling that Papa, being so unworldly, was the last person to negotiate anything as regards finance.

But women were not supposed to interest themselves in such matters and Atalanta was aware that neither the Earl nor William would see any reason why they should impress with their munificence a man they had always quite openly despised.

They were almost at the Castle gates before Atalanta managed to ask the question which had been in her mind ever since she had walked into the Drawing Room.

"Mama," she said suddenly, "why is Cousin William marrying me?"

She knew by the way her Mother hesitated before she replied that Lady Evelyn was choosing her words carefully.

"He said he had always been fond of you, Atalanta," she replied.

"That is not true!" Atalanta answered. "I cannot remember his speaking to me except to tell me and Cicely to get out of his way and go upstairs."

"Then you must ask him yourself," Lady Evelyn said quickly. "I am sure, Atalanta, you will find his explanation very satisfactory."

Atalanta gave a little sigh.

She was not going to find the truth there, but she knew by the swiftness of the events taking place that somehow she must learn the answer to her question.

They reached the Castle and Atalanta was aware the moment they stepped in through the front door that the staff knew of her new status.

The Butler's bow to both Lady Evelyn and the Vicar

was very much lower and more impressive than he had ever accorded them in the past.

The two maids in the big bedroom, where Atalanta and Lady Evelyn left their cloaks, attended them so assiduously and spent so much time fluffing out their gowns and touching up their hair, that, for the first time since she had been coming to the Castle, Atalanta felt an honoured guest.

The bedroom was on the first floor and Cicely slept in a room at the end of the corridor.

"Wait for me one moment, Mama," Atalanta pleaded. "I just want to speak to Cicely."

"Do not be long, darling," Lady Evelyn replied. "It must be nearly five minutes to eight and you know your Uncle hates to be kept waiting."

"I will not be more than a second, Mama," Atalanta promised, and picking up her skirts she ran down the corridor.

She had reached the bedroom door and was just opening it when she heard someone call her name and saw her Aunt coming down the corridor behind her.

Glittering with jewels and with a tiara in her grey hair, which she wore even when dining alone with the Earl, Louise Winchcombe was, at sixty, still an extremely good-looking woman.

She had, however, a cold, hard manner which frightened most of those with whom she came into contact, and there were few among her contemporaries whom she might have called a close friend.

"Good evening, Atalanta!" she said.

"Good evening, Aunt Louise," Atalanta replied, dropping her a curtsey.

It seemed to her as if her Aunt's eyes were flickering over Clementine's old dress with contempt. Then she said, in the cold manner in which she habitually spoke:

"William has told me that you are engaged. I hope you realise what a lucky young woman you are to have won such an exceptionally brilliant husband?"

"Yes, Aunt Louise."

Her aunt always had the power of making Atalanta feel tongue-tied and incredibly stupid.

"You were about to visit Cicely, I think," the Countess went on. "She has not yet been told the good news. We will tell her together."

She opened the bedroom door as she spoke. Cicely was lying flat, without a pillow, in the big bed which always made her seem small and pathetic.

"Hello, Mama!" she exclaimed, and added as she saw Atalanta, "What a surprise! I did not know you were dining here tonight."

"Atalanta has some special news to tell you," her mother said. "William has asked her to be his wife."

There was a little pause, then Cicely said: "How lovely! Now Atalanta will be my sister-in-law."

She spoke with apparent spontaneity, but Atalanta, who knew every intonation of Cicely's voice, was suddenly aware that she was acting.

Cicely had known already of William's proposal; she was certain of it.

"We must go down to dinner," the Countess said. "It is nearly eight o'clock. You two girls will have time to talk about everything tomorrow. Now Cicely must go to sleep."

"It is very exciting!" Cicely said. "I am so glad, Atalanta!"

"I will see you tomorrow," Atalanta said.

She bent down as she spoke to kiss Cicely's cheek, and as she did so she heard Cicely say, in a soft whisper, "I have so much to tell you!"

Atalanta followed her Aunt to the door. As she reached it, she turned back to look at Cicely and saw her wink. Then she closed the door and moved downstairs after the Countess.

Dinner was a slow and pompous ceremony, as Atalanta had grown to expect at the Castle, but not so dreary as usual. The Chef had made a special effort because William was present, and Clementine was in extraordinarily good spirits.

31

It was only when the ladies withdrew from the Dining Room that Atalanta learnt the reason for this.

"I do not suppose," the Countess said to Lady Evelyn, "that William had time to tell you that we are expecting a very important guest tomorrow."

"I think he spoke only of Atalanta," Lady Evelyn replied.

"Then I must tell you that we are expecting a visit from the Duc d'Abencom," the Countess said. "You may have heard of him. He is the cousin and close friend of Prince Alexander of Vallon!"

"I thought that Vallon, after being occupied by the Germans, had been annexed by the French after the withdrawal of the Germans," Lady Evelyn remarked.

"You are right," the Countess agreed. "It is extraordinary, Evelyn, how well informed you manage to be, despite the life you lead."

"We do not have to turn into turnips even if we do live in Little Combe," Lady Evelyn said, the colour rising in her face.

Her sister-in-law's sneers about her position in life invariably, try as she might, got under her skin.

"William has brought us great news," the Countess continued. "Vallon is to be reinstated as an independent Principality."

"Oh, I am glad!" Lady Evelyn exclaimed. "I always resented the idea of that poor little country being deprived of its independence. It was so unfair."

"Great Britain has been largely instrumental, so William tells me, in persuading the French Government to right the injustice," the Countess went on, "and it has been suggested to Prince Alexander that an English wife would be most acceptable to the Foreign Office, if, as is expected, Vallon will look to this country for further support and benefits."

"An English wife," Lady Evelyn echoed.

"The Duc will discuss with us the possibility of a marriage between the Prince and Clementine."

"How wonderful!" Lady Evelyn exclaimed. "And how proud you must be!"

"I have always thought of Clementine as being Royal," the Countess said smugly. "With her beauty, she is too good for the average commoner, however well bred, or a nobleman, however important his rank. William assures me that Prince Alexander is extremely presentable. Anyway, we shall hear more when the Duc arrives tomorrow."

"Yes, of course," Lady Evelyn agreed.

"It will mean that I shall be obliged to take Clementine to Paris very shortly," the Countess went on, "and William has asked that Atalanta shall accompany us."

Atalanta, who had taken no part in the conversation until now, sat up suddenly in her chair.

"You mean I can come to Paris with you, Aunt Louise?"

"That is what I have just said, Atalanta, if you have been listening carefully," the Countess replied. "I personally consider it quite unnecessary for you to make the journey, but William is *insistent*."

She accented the word.

"He wishes to present you to his friends—on the continent—with whom he has been working these past years. You should therefore be ready to accompany me in perhaps a week's time, if not sooner."

"But Louise!" Lady Evelyn ejaculated. "Atalanta has no clothes."

"I am well aware of that," the Countess remarked acidly. "William has already spoken to me of the manner in which Atalanta was dressed when he called at the Vicarage this evening."

They heard the contempt in her voice.

"I shall be going to London immediately the Duc leaves to purchase some gowns for Clementine and myself. I will also choose some dresses for Atalanta, and tomorrow I will send to the Vicarage a number of things which Clementine will no longer require. I imagine you can get them altered in time?"

33

"If they are not too outdated," Lady Evelyn said with a flash of spirit which Atalanta had not expected from her. "Then I imagine we can get them done."

The Countess pursed her lips, and Atalanta realised she was about to make some scathing and crushing retort, when the door opened and the gentlemen joined the ladies.

There was an apologetic expression on her Father's face which told Atalanta all too clearly that he had been brow-beaten by the Earl.

As if Lady Evelyn sensed it too, she went immediately to his side and put her hand on his arm as if by being close to him she made him realise that nothing mattered save that they were together—ready to defy their families as they had defied them so many years ago.

"We must not keep you up late," Lady Evelyn said to her half brother.

"Quite right!" the Earl boomed. "Early to bed and early to rise has always been my motto. Cannot stand this modern habit of coming downstairs when the day is half-over. You will remember, Evelyn, when we were children, breakfast was at seven."

"Yes, indeed," Lady Evelyn answered, "and very cold it used to be on a winter's morning when we had to break the ice on the water jugs in our bedrooms."

"Made us hardy!" the Earl retorted. "Shall I send for the carriage?"

"Yes, please, Lionel," Lady Evelyn replied.

William moved across the room to Atalanta.

"I have something to show you," he said and, walking ahead, opened the door into an Ante-Room which opened off the Drawing Room.

The room seemed dark and was rather cold, as only two gas lamps were lit and no candles. As William turned in the centre of the room to face Atalanta, the shadows on his face seemed to make him older than he had looked in the brightly lit Drawing Room.

"What is it?" she asked.

She had the sudden feeling that he intended to withdraw the proposal of marriage he had made earlier in the day, but in answer he drew from his pocket a small velvet-lined case.

"When you come to Paris," he said, "I will wish you to wear a ring on your finger."

He opened the case and Atalanta, seeing the ring, recognised it immediately.

It was one the Countess often wore. It had a large emerald in the centre and a number of small diamonds on either side of it.

"Is that my engagement ring?" she asked.

"I hope it will please you," he said stiffly.

She felt she was being ungracious and said quickly: "Thank you! Thank you . . . it is very magnificent!"

"I am sure you will find that everyone will think so," he answered.

He took her hand in his and put the ring on her third finger.

"Mama will help you with your clothes, Atalanta. You have a lot to learn, but I know you will find my life and my career a very interesting one."

"I am sure I shall," Atalanta answered.

She wanted to ask him why he was marrying her. She felt the words actually on her lips and then, before she could speak, he kissed her cheek lightly.

She felt his lips were cold.

Then she told herself she was imagining it. His touch had been so light, so perfunctory, that she could not possibly have known anything except that it was a gesture of affection.

Already William had turned away towards the door into the Drawing Room and had opened it.

"We must not keep the horses waiting," he said.

"No, of course not," Atalanta said meekly.

She walked back into the Drawing Room. Her Father and Mother were waiting at the fireside. She knew by the smile on her mother's face that she thought William had taken her away because he wished to speak of his affection.

Then abruptly, because she felt embarrassed, Atalanta held out her hand with the ring on it.

"Oh, your engagement ring!" Lady Evelyn said. "How lovely—how very splendid!"

Then, as she too recognised it, she looked towards her sister-in-law.

"It is kind of you, Louise, to part with something you so often wear."

"It has always been one of William's favourite rings," the Countess said coldly.

"The carriage is at the door, M'Lady," the Butler announced from the doorway.

"Come along, come along," the Earl said. "Must not keep the horses waiting. I do not often take them out at night, but this evening is a special occasion."

"Yes, of course," Lady Evelyn said, "and we are very grateful, Lionel."

Atalanta dutifully kissed her Aunt on the cheek, then her uncle, and held out her hand to William.

He raised it to his lips, but it was only a gesture and she thought at that moment how Paul Beaulieu's mouth had been warm against her skin.

"I have had my hand kissed twice today," she thought, "and the first time it meant something."

She wondered what it would be like to kiss William on the lips and felt herself shiver.

There was something about the hard line of his mouth which made it impossible to imagine him kissing anyone, least of all herself.

"You will give to the man you love your heart, your body and your soul!"

She could hear Paul Beaulieu's voice speaking. He had made her feel as if her breath was constricted in her throat.

Would she even want to give William her heart, her body, and her soul?

"Why does he want to marry me?" The question seemed to repeat itself over and over again in rhythm with the sound of the horses' hooves carrying them down the drive and back towards the village.

Both Lady Evelyn and the Vicar were silent, and Atalanta realised that her mother was tired.

It had been a long and difficult evening, but dinner parties at the Castle were always stiff and uncomfortable. One always came away wondering if one had said the wrong thing, or too much or too little.

Supposing, Atalanta thought with a sudden sense of horror, that all her dinners in the future when she was with William were like tonight.

He had hardly spoken to her, but then there had been little chance for him to do so, even though he had sat next to her at dinner.

His Father had monopolised the conversation—droning on about the iniquities of the Government where the country's agricultural needs were concerned, declaring against the ungratefulness of the farm workers, and predicting that Britain would soon be swamped with cheap food from abroad which would make British farmers bankrupt within a few years.

Everyone at the table had heard the Earl's opinions on these matters innumerable times before, so much so that no one had made any effort to argue or to do anything but agree with His Lordship.

Atalanta, stealing a glance at her cousin William, had seen that he looked bored and cynical.

No wonder he stayed abroad, she thought! He could not find it very amusing at the Castle, hearing his Father still airing the same grievances he had been forced to listen to on his last visit.

She wondered what William's interests were. She longed to ask him if when he was in Paris he had seen any of the Impressionist paintings.

Then she realised that to admit that she had even heard of anything so controversial might in some way involve Paul Beaulieu and the fact that he was painting a picture in the woods.

She therefore said nothing, but she found herself

thinking, as she undressed for bed, not of William and the big emerald ring which lay on her dressing table, but of Paul Beaulieu and how he had said she was lovely.

Did he really think so, she wondered, or was it just the flattery which she felt came easily to every Frenchman's lips?

How little she knew about them, she thought, except what she had read. She loved reading in French to Cicely and she had searched the big Library at the Castle for books which she knew would amuse her.

They had seemed a dull lot until, one day, Atalanta had entered William's sitting room, which adjoined his bedroom in the West Wing.

It was always kept ready for his return and contained trophies that he had won at school, photographs taken of himself and his friends at Oxford, and to her delight a large number of books far more up to date than those in the Library downstairs.

She had quite shamelessly taken a number of them and hidden them in a locked cupboard in Cicely's bedroom.

The Countess, who seldom read, would not perhaps have realised the implications of Atalanta reading aloud *Madame Bovary* to Cicely, but the girls took no chances.

There was always another book open on the bed when Atalanta was reading a volume from William's shelves, and it was quite easy at the first sound of a footstep outside to slip a book which might have offended or caused a storm of disapproval under the bedclothes!

"Does Paul Beaulieu talk like the characters in a French novel?" Atalanta asked herself.

It was difficult to know the answer. When he spoke to her in his deep voice, it was hard to believe that he was anything but sincere.

"Is it possible she could be more beautiful than you?" he had asked when they spoke of Clementine. And later he had enquired: "Are the men in this part of England all blind?"

Then again she felt her heart leap as she remembered how he had put down his palette and stared at her.

"You are a very remarkable person," he had said, "besides being utterly and completely lovely."

She had not until this moment, in the darkness of her own bed, dared to repeat these words even to herself, but now she could hear his voice saying them so clearly that it was almost as if he was there beside her.

Then she shut her eyes.

"I have to think of William," she told herself. "I am to marry him. I am to be his wife!"

It did not seem real; she could not make herself believe it was really happening. It was not as if she felt she moved in a dream, but rather in a nightmare from which she could not awake.

Atalanta found it almost impossible to sleep.

She heard the Church clock strike nearly every hour of the night. She wondered where Paul Beaulieu was staying. The Inn in Little Combe was small and very uncomfortable.

Perhaps he was in the next village, where there was a Posting Inn which was sometimes patronised by the local gentry when they were fox hunting. That was where he would be, she thought.

At six o'clock, still without sound sleep although she had dozed a little between the hours, Atalanta rose.

She dressed herself in one of her best gowns. It was not much better than the one she had worn the day before, but if William came to see her she hoped that she would not again be embarrassed by that look of contempt in his eyes.

She did her hair carefully, put on an apron to protect her gown, then went downstairs.

The house was quiet and shrouded in darkness. Her Father and Mother and the twins were still asleep. The maid from the village, who had only been at the Vicarage for a month, was still in her bedroom, although she should have started work at least half an hour earlier.

"It is no use," Atalanta thought. "The village girls will never wake unless someone takes a cold sponge to them."

She did not blame them; for they were little more than children and got very tired trying to remember all the things they had never been taught in their cottage homes.

Atalanta opened the garden door and went outside. The world seemed very fresh, and the sunshine was pale gold like her hair as it spread up the sky behind the beech trees which grew just outside the Vicarage garden.

There were lilacs, purple and white against a red-brick wall and she wished suddenly that Paul Beaulieu could see them.

The colours seemed vivid in the early morning light—Impressionists' colours with no black, fluid and strangely luminous. She began to count the hours until she could see him again.

There were however innumerable things for her to do. Besides feeding the chickens and the horses, it was Atalanta's job to groom the mare her Father rode, the old cob which drew the pony cart, and Robin, the horse she shared with the twins.

They took it in turns to go riding, and as she brushed him down Atalanta could not help thinking how wonderful it would be to have a horse of her own—a thoroughbred, a horse such as Clementine rode.

Sometimes when the Earl was in a very good mood, he mounted Bernard in the holidays, but these special treats only seemed to make Bernard even more dissatisfied with poor Robin.

"He is as slow as an old mule," he had said plaintively to Lady Evelyn at Easter when he was down from Oxford. "Can I try to find a better animal at the Horse Fair?"

"No, darling, I am sorry, we just cannot afford it,"

his Mother replied. "If only Papa's new book were to be a success!"

"If we wait for that we shall wait until Doomsday," Bernard retorted, and then seeing the hurt in Lady Evelyn's face he put his arm round her and kissed her.

"I am sorry, Mama; do not listen to my grumbles. It is unkind and you have enough troubles without my adding to them."

"I would so love you to have a really good mount," Lady Evelyn said. "Shall I speak to your Uncle and ask him as a favour to let you ride his horses?"

"No, no," Bernard said quickly, "do not ask him now. He will think he is being so magnanimous that I shall not get a day's hunting in the winter. If you are going to go on your knees before him, do it then. Why they cannot be generous and let me ride some of those under-exercised animals in the Castle stables, I cannot think."

"I am sure Lionel does not mean to be so selfish," Lady Evelyn said, almost under her breath.

"It is just bred in him!" Bernard said with a grin, and kissed her again as she tried to expostulate.

"It is all right, Mama, I have been asked to stay with one of my Oxford friends next vacation. He has a huge estate in Ireland and a dozen horses I can ride to my heart's content."

"Oh, that will be wonderful for you," Lady Evelyn exclaimed.

"It is not really the same as being at home," Bernard said warm-heartedly and Atalanta had seen the gladness in her Mother's eyes.

When she had finished grooming the horses, there were magazines to be delivered in the village, a notice to be put up in the Church porch, and the Vestry to be tidied after the Church Wardens' meeting.

The morning passed so quickly that Atalanta was quite surprised to find it was time for luncheon.

The twins, who had been having lessons with a retired teacher in the village, came rushing back to the house.

They had seen Atalanta's engagement ring before they had left and it was only as they began to talk about it, speculating as to how much it was worth, that she remembered guiltily she had not thought about the ring since she had taken it off the night before.

"Do not forget to put it on before you go up to the Castle," Lady Evelyn reminded her. "I am sure William would be very hurt if you forgot his present."

"It is really more of a present from Aunt Louise," Atalanta said.

"William would not have had time to buy you anything himself, would he?" Lady Evelyn replied with unanswerable logic. "In fact it is quite usual for a son to give his bride one of the family jewels. After all, your Aunt Louise has so much jewelery it would be quite ridiculous for William to buy more. Anyway, I am sure later he will give you a special engagement present he chooses himself when you get to Paris."

"If I am going to Paris, I had better remind Aunt Louise about the clothes that have to be altered," Atalanta said as she rose from the luncheon table.

"Paris—what is this about Paris?" Chryseis asked.

And then the twins were screaming with excitement as Atalanta explained that she was to leave England in a week's time.

"You are lucky, Atalanta! I wish you could take us, too."

There was something so wistful in the way Hebe spoke that Atalanta instinctively put out her arms.

"One day perhaps I will be able to take you," she said. "Would it not be marvellous if we can all go together? Think of visiting the Louvre, walking along by the Seine, and seeing Notre Dame. We would have such fun!"

"Yes, we would," Hebe agreed. "Why can we not all go? But even if we cannot, now that Atalanta is going to marry William she can find us eligible husbands as soon as we are old enough. A Duke apiece would be just what we each want! Would it not, Chryseis? Although as far as I am concerned, I would settle for a Marquis or an Earl."

"I cannot think what Papa would say if he heard you talking like that," Lady Evelyn said repressively.

"Do not pretend, Mama," Chryseis said. "You are delighted that Atalanta is to be a Viscountess. I wonder if Aunt Louise will part with one of her tiaras. She would not like doing so. But perhaps Cousin William will persuade her. After all, he got the ring out of her!"

"Chryseis, I will not have you talking in such a vulgar manner!" Lady Evelyn said sharply, and this time Chryseis was shamed into silence.

Atalanta reached the Castle half an hour before she was due. Cicely was expecting her, and her eyes lit up as Atalanta came into the bedroom and shut the door behind her.

"I knew you would be early." She smiled.

Atalanta crossed the room, kissed Cicely's cheek, and sat down near the bed.

"Tell me all you know."

To her surprise, Cicely hesitated a moment.

"Do you want to know the truth?" she asked. "Or what sounds nice?"

"You know we have always told each other the truth," Atalanta replied.

"You will not like it," Cicely said, "at least I do not think you will."

"I want to know why he is marrying me," Atalanta answered. "You know the answer, do you not?"

Cicely nodded her head slowly.

"I was sure of that last night," Atalanta said.

"I do not think Mama was suspicious," Cicely remarked.

"Of what?" Atalanta enquired.

"That I knew exactly what had happened," Cicely answered. "You see, she thought I was asleep."

"Tell me! Tell me everything from the very beginning," Atalanta pleaded.

"You remember yesterday," Cicely began, "when Nurse came in and said that you were to leave because I had to rest earlier than usual, because William was coming home?"

"Yes, I remember," Atalanta answered.

"He had sent a telegram saying he would arrive in the evening. Mama was in a tremendous flap from the moment the telegram arrived."

"I can understand that," Atalanta said. "Aunt Louise is devoted to William."

"I think he is the only person she does care about," Cicely said. "Anyway, I was taken down as usual to rest on the balcony outside her bedroom, the canopy was erected over me, and Nurse said I was to try and sleep."

She made a grimace.

"Mama in her bedroom was changing into her afternoon gown," she went on, "and as she wanted me to sleep, she did not talk. I was really just dropping off when I heard the door open and Mama exclaim, 'William, we were not expecting you until this evening!'"

Cicely had learnt from the many books which Atalanta had read to her how to express herself. The story she told Atalanta was very eloquent. . . .

"I managed to get an earlier boat, Mama," William explained as he crossed the room.

"How well you look, my dear boy," the Countess exclaimed, "and so smart!"

"It would be impossible to be anything else in Paris," William replied. "But listen, Mama, I have a great deal to say to you and very little time in which to do it."

"You are not staying long?"

"No, I am returning to Paris almost immediately. Very exciting things are happening there, which is why I need your help."

"My help?" the Countess questioned.

"Yes, Mama, I need a wife!"

"A wife! Are you joking?"

"No indeed, Mama, I am extremely serious."

"I cannot believe it!" the Countess exlaimed. "You

know you have always said you would never marry, and
we all know it is the fault of that . . . woman who has
done her best to ruin your life."

"This is not the time, Mama, to talk about Lady
Trenton."

"It is over? You are no longer infatuated with her?"
the Countess asked.

"I have no intention of talking about my private af-
fairs," William replied. "We went through all this three
years ago when you and Papa made it very clear that
so long as my liaison continued you did not wish to see
me at the Castle."

"That was not my decision," the Countess said quickly.
"You know, William, that I love you and all I want is
your happiness."

"Well, now you can help me be happy by finding me
a wife. And I must have one at once."

"I shall be delighted if you wish to marry!" the Countess exclaimed. "But why must I find you a wife? Surely that is something you should decide for yourself."

Her son walked across the bedroom and back again.

"I will be frank with you, Mama," he said. "I know
no young girls. I have not, these past three years, moved
in the sort of society, as you are well aware, where I
am likely to meet them. My friends are gay and glam-
orous, but they are all married and those who are
not are certainly not the type of wife I should choose
for a future Ambassador."

"William! Do you mean . . . there is a chance?"

"There is not only a chance, Mama, it is a certainty.
That is why it is vitally important that you should find
me a wife and that I should go back to Paris if not
actually married—then engaged."

"But why? Do explain!" his mother begged.

William hesitated a moment before he began.

"You know, Mama, that I have been working with
Sir Heatherington Houghton on the restoration of Independence to the Principality of Vallon. Sir Heatherington was, as you know, the Ambassador in Vallon before

it was overrun by the Germans and later annexed by the French."

He paused before he continued solemnly.

"We pleaded, we argued, we brought every possible pressure to bear on the French Government. It seemed as if they were adamant.

"Then, last year, a new President was elected, Monsieur Jules Grévy. He has proved unexpectedly sympathetic to our cause. Vallon is to be given back its Independence and Royal status and the French assent will be signed next week."

"William, how splendid! How delighted you must be!"

"A little more than delighted, Mama. Sir Heatherington has informed me that he wishes to retire now that his task is completed. He will be seventy next year and it is not surprising that he feels too old to carry on. He will make a strong representation to the Foreign Office that I should succeed him."

"William, you will be an Ambassador!"

"The youngest Ambassador in Europe, Mama, and you know what that means. The first step Vallon, the next Vienna, Rome, or Paris! You may well be proud of me!"

"I am indeed proud of you, my dear. More proud than I can possibly say."

"But, Mama, an Ambassador has to be married. At least as far as Vallon is concerned. The Foreign Office would not consider an unmarried man a suitable envoy at this particular moment in a country which will have to build up its constitution."

The Countess put up her hands to her forehead.

"But, William, where can I find you a bride?"

"That is not all, Mama. I have something else to tell you. Sir Heatherington has repeatedly recommended to the Council of Vallon, and to the Prince himself, that as Great Britain has given so much help and support and has promised a great many trade concessions in the future to Vallon, it would be tremendously advantageous to the country if Prince Alexander were to take an English wife."

The Countess gave an exclamation and clasped her hands together.

"Sir Heatherington, if you remember, met Clementine when he was last in London," her son continued. "Not surprisingly he thought her very beautiful and he has suggested, and I have concurred, that the Prince's cousin, the Duc d'Abencom, should come here immediately and talk with you and Papa of the possibility of Clementine espousing Prince Alexander."

"Oh, William, how wonderful! It is everything I always hoped for—that Clementine should be a Princess, that she should be Royal and take her place amongst the reigning families of Europe. It is something I have always dreamt would be right for her."

"All you have to do, Mama, is to agree to everything the Duc suggests and to bring Clementine to Paris as speedily as possible."

"Surely we must have time to consider this."

"There is no time!" William said firmly. "There is no time as far as Clementine is concerned, because once it is known that Prince Alexander is to be reinstated, half the Royal houses of Europe will be offering him their daughters.

"As regards myself, Mama, I must have a wife, or rather the promise of one, before I return to Paris tomorrow or, at the very latest, the next day."

"William, it is impossible! Who is there? Let me think! There is the eldest Somerton girl, but you know as well as I do, Lord Somerton would not hear of your courting her at such an unseemly speed. He is very stiff and straight-laced where his daughters are concerned."

"I have seen the Somerton girl, Mama. She must be nearly thirty and has a face like a horse, which is not surprising as all she thinks about is hunting. I would not marry her if she were the last female left in England."

"Well, there is Lord Loveday's daughter, but she has

not yet made her début. You cannot marry a girl from the Schoolroom."

"Stop telling me who I cannot have, Mama, and start telling me who there is," William said. "Clementine must have some friends."

"You will need somebody well-bred and someone of whom you will not be ashamed," his mother remarked, "but I cannot imagine anyone of importance allowing their daughter to become engaged to a man she has not even met, and whom she has only heard of by reputation."

There was an innuendo in his mother's voice that William could not ignore.

"Is Lady Trenton still sticking in your throat, Mama? I promise you that is finished! Actually it was over six months ago."

"Oh, William, I am so glad!"

"And now back to the list of prospective wives," William prompted.

"I cannot think—there is really no one—" the Countess began. Then she gave a little gasp. It is not ideal . . . but at least she comes from a good family."

"And who is that?" William asked.

"Atalanta! Your cousin Atalanta, poor Evelyn's child. She is nineteen and has grown quite pretty. Of course Evelyn spoils her children quite absurdly, but Atalanta is well educated. She speaks languages, which should be an asset to an Ambassador's wife."

"I remember her," William said abruptly. "If there is no one else, Mama, she will have to do. As you say she is well bred, and perhaps it is not such a bad idea to marry someone who will be grateful to me and who will certainly not dare to complain of my past misdemeanours."

"I cannot believe that any girl would do that," the Countess replied sharply.

"I will go down to the Vicarage as soon as I have seen Papa," William said. "This means I can get back to

Paris at once, and you can bring Atalanta over with you when you bring Clementine."

Bending and kissing his Mother's cheek, he went from the room and Cicely heard the door shut behind him.

There was silence in the bedroom and then she heard her Mother give a sudden exclamation. There was the rustle of silken skirts and Cicely shut her eyes.

She knew her Mother was standing at the end of the couch, looking down at her.

"Cicely," the Countess said very softly, "are you awake?"

Cicely did not stir. After a moment her Mother went back into the bedroom, apparently satisfied.

"Now you understand," Cicely said to Atalanta.

"Yes, I understand," Atalanta said slowly. "I could not imagine why he should want to marry me."

Chapter Three

ATALANTA, walking across the park, found herself moving more and more slowly towards the wood.

She wanted to see Paul Beaulieu; at the same time she knew an inexpressible reluctance at having to explain to him what had happened.

She told herself it was ridiculous that she should talk to him at all about what was entirely a private family affair, and yet for some extraordinary reason she knew she must tell him everything—a Stranger whom she had not known until yesterday.

She left Cicely early because she wanted to spend more time in the wood, only to find the Butler waiting in the Hall to inform her that the Countess wished to speak to her in the Boudoir.

A little apprehensively, Atalanta entered the room to find her Aunt writing letters at her desk in front of one of the windows.

"Oh, there you are, Atalanta," she said. "I have a message for you from William."

"Has he left?" Atalanta asked in surprise.

She had half-wanted to see William again and half-feared being alone with him. She could not explain her feelings even to herself.

"William has already returned to Paris," her aunt said, "and our plans are changed. The Duc is arriving this evening and I received a letter from him this morning saying that he intends to travel back to Paris on Friday and suggesting we accompany him."

"On Friday!" Atalanta cried. "But that is the day after tomorrow!"

"I am well aware of that, Atalanta," her Aunt replied, "but it would of course be much more pleasant to have the Duc as our escort. We shall therefore, all three of us, leave with him early on Friday."

"But, Aunt Louise, I have no clothes," Atalanta protested.

"If you had allowed me to finish what I was saying, Atalanta," her Aunt Louise said sternly, "you would have learnt that I have already sent my maid to London to collect some gowns for Clementine and myself. I have also told her to bring back for you a traveling dress and cloak, a day gown, and one for the evening. The rest of the things you will require we can purchase in Paris."

"Oh, thank you, Aunt Louise!" Atalanta exclaimed.

"What is more, the pony cart has already left for the Vicarage with a large trunkful of Clementine's clothes. Your Mother will not have time to alter all of them, but there is no reason why they cannot be dispatched later. I suggest that you go home now and help her with as many things as possible."

"Yes, Aunt Louise," Atalanta said meekly.

Perhaps her tone was too meek for the Countess glanced at her sharply.

"I hope you realise how very fortunate you are," she said. "There are not many girls in your position who not only have the chance of marrying someone as important, as clever, and as charming as William, but also have their trousseau provided for them."

She looked Atalanta up and down before she continued.

"I quite see that it would be impossible for your Mother in her straitened circumstances to dress you as befits the wife of a future Ambassador."

"It is very kind of you," Atalanta said. "Thank you very much."

"Well, that will be all," the Countess said sharply. "Do as I say, Atalanta; hurry home and I shall not expect you to visit Cicely tomorrow. You will be busy packing. When the gowns arrive from London, I will send them to you. I am sure that I can trust Madame Yvette, who has looked after Clementine for so long, to find you something both suitable and attractive. We would not wish William to be ashamed of you, would we?"

It was only when she was outside the Castle that Atalanta gave a deep sigh as if dispelling some of her tension and indeed some of the temper she had felt rising dangerously when her Aunt had been speaking to her.

It was always the same. The Countess never missed an opportunity of making her feel small and insignificant, and also of making it very clear that she despised her Mother for taking a penniless, unimportant Vicar as her husband and the father of her children.

Atalanta had walked quite a little way before she felt her anger subside and then it was the thought of Paul waiting for her which made her slow her steps.

"What will he think of this marriage?" she wondered.

Then she asked herself how could it possibly matter one way or another what he thought.

Paul was waiting for her, but not, as she had expected, where he had painted her inside the wood. Instead he was leaning against one of the pine trees at the edge of the park.

She realised that he must have seen her long before she saw him and was suddenly conscious that her hair was blown in the wind and her cheeks a little flushed.

Would she still appear as a Goddess to him, she wondered, or, like William, would he be critical of her untidiness and the fact that her gown, although it was her best, was distinctly out of fashion?

She reached his side, looked up at him, and knew from the expression in his eyes that to him she was not a shabby inconsequential girl from the Vicarage.

"You were walking very slowly," he said before she could speak. "I began to think you would never get here."

He put out his hand as he spoke and Atalanta put her right hand into his. She felt the strength of his fingers as he raised it to his lips.

Then he said unexpectedly:

"What has upset you?"

She had not thought he would be so perceptive and, taking her hand quickly from his, she moved ahead of him into the wood.

"I want to see my picture," she said.

He did not answer her and they walked through the trees until they came to his easel. She stood looking at the canvas, her eyes wide and a little surprised.

She had not known exactly what she expected.

She could not remember ever having seen a portrait done by an Impressionist. Her eyes on the canvas looked out wonderingly, surprised, yet with a strange depth in them.

She had thought to see herself silhouetted against the pine trees; instead the background seemed only to be a luminous mist out of which her face loomed compellingly and painted in tiny little strokes, quite differently from any portrait she had ever seen before.

There were no hard outlines, no contours. The whole picture seemed fluid, as if Paul Beaulieu had caught her in a moment of movement. Yet she knew that was not the explanation.

She stood looking at it for a long time and then, at last, she said: "I think . . . you are trying to say that I am . . . unsure of myself. That I am looking at life . . . not exactly taking part in it. Perhaps I am not fully . . .

aware of what living should . . . mean and yet I know
it is very . . . exciting and . . . very beautiful."

She spoke almost as if she were explaining his picture
to herself, rather than to him, and it made her start when
he spoke and she realised that he was so close to her,
even closer than she thought he would be.

"You are unique and quite perfect! What can I say
except that I love you?"

Atalanta stood very still, feeling that she had not
heard him correctly.

Then he took her hand, the one closest to him, and
would have raised it to his lips. As he moved it, he
saw the large emerald ring on her third finger.

He was very still and Atalanta, because she was embarrassed, said quickly: "I was just going to . . . tell
you. Yesterday after I left you, when I returned home
. . . my Cousin William was . . . there. He had asked
. . . Papa for my hand . . . in marriage."

"And you accepted him?"

"Papa and Mama had accepted for . . . me. They
were very pleased. They think that I am very lucky to
have the chance of . . . marrying someone so . . . important and so . . . clever."

Paul still held her hand. She took it away almost
roughly and, turning, walked towards the felled tree on
which she had sat for her portrait.

"Can you not . . . understand what it will . . . mean?"
she asked. "I will be able to help Bernard who is at
Oxford. He has no pocket money, practically nothing to
spend on himself or with which to entertain his friends!
And if, as I expect, I shall have horses to ride . . .
Bernard could ride them too in the holidays."

Paul did not speak and Atalanta did not look at him,
and yet she knew that he was looking at her, standing
quite still by the easel.

"And the twins are very . . . excited as you can . . .
imagine," she went on in a hurried, breathless little
voice. "They are already planning parties to which I
will be able to . . . take them. They will be able to

have my clothes . . . not when they are worn out and old-fashioned like the ones I get from Clementine . . . but up to date. Besides I will be able to give them . . . new things as . . . well."

Still Paul said nothing. As if she must convince him, Atalanta continued almost desperately.

"If indeed the Marriage Settlement is a good one . . . although I doubt if Uncle Lionel will be generous . . . I could pay for a Curate to help Papa with his parish work. All he really wants to do is to work at his books. They are good, they are clever!

She gave a little sigh.

"Everyone who has read them says they are brilliant, but they make so very little money. It is only a few libraries and scholars who buy them, and if I could afford . . . help for Papa, then he would have more time to write."

Her voice died away. It seemed to her as if it was swallowed up in the quiet of the wood. Then as she waited, Paul asked: "And you? Have you thought about yourself?"

"What do you mean?"

"You know quite well what I am asking," he replied. "Do you love this man? Does he love you?"

"How could I love anyone I have not seen for three years?" Atalanta asked. "And as for William loving me . . . he has to have a wife. He is to be the Ambassador to Vallon and he cannot be appointed unless he is a . . . married man."

"Vallon?" Paul questioned.

"Perhaps I should not tell you—I believe it is a secret at the moment—but Vallon is to receive its Independence again. It will become a Principality as it was before, and William is to be our Ambassador there."

"A very enviable position," Paul said and Atalanta heard the irony in his voice.

"He will be the youngest Ambassador in Europe."

"And you? You will enjoy being an Ambassador's wife?"

"I expect . . . so," Atalanta answered, but there was no elation in her voice.

"And do you think," Paul asked very quietly, "that all the pretty gowns you will wear, all the parties you will go to, all the compliments you will receive because you are young and beautiful, will make up for love?"

"What . . . do you mean?" Atalanta asked in a whisper.

"I told you yesterday," he answered, "that one day, Little Atalanta, you will love someone with your heart, your body and your soul. Is that what you feel for Cousin William?"

"You are . . . not to speak to . . . me like . . . this," Atalanta murmured. "There is nothing I can do about it . . . nothing! Papa and Mama are so pleased! It will make all the difference to them and even if they had asked me . . . it would have been . . . impossible for me to say . . . no."

"You are wrong," Paul said. "It would not be impossible, merely brave. I thought, Atalanta, that you had a lot of courage."

"I am not . . . brave enough to make Mama . . . unhappy," Atalanta answered. "I have never seen her look so young! She says she has never regretted marrying Papa . . . but once I asked her if she had ever been sorry that she turned down the Duke of Loth. . . ."

Atalanta's voice died away.

"And what did your Mother answer?" Paul prompted.

"She said," Atalanta went on, " 'Women are so vulnerable! You see, darling, if anything happened to Papa I should have nothing. But if anything happened to me Papa would have his writing. It means so much to him.' I think she meant me to realise . . . it is not always . . . wise to give up . . . everything for . . . love."

There was a little silence and then Paul said:

"Do you believe in love at first sight?"

Atalanta glanced at him almost for the first time since she had been talking to him. Her eyes were very wide and troubled and then, as they met his, she was unable to look away.

She felt as if he held her close to him, that she was his captive, although he was not touching her.

"I thought it was a myth, something novelists imagined might happen," he said in his deep voice, "but when yesterday as I watched a small Goddess come walking across the park in the sunshine, something very strange happened to my heart."

He paused.

"Later, when you talked to me, Atalanta, and when you sat where you are sitting now, I knew that you had walked into my life and I should never be free of you."

"It is . . . not . . . true," she said, almost beneath her breath. "You are . . . imagining it."

"Do you really think that?" he asked.

She wanted to look away from him, but she could not. She felt herself held spellbound by that strange magic she had known yesterday, but now it was more intense, a burning fire which she knew was dangerous but from which she could not escape.

"I love you, Atalanta," Paul said. "I have thought about you all night; I thought this morning while I waited to see you would never pass. It seemed a century until you came to me."

"You must not . . . say such . . . things to . . . me."

"Why not?" he asked. "I am a man, an ordinary man like any other and I have the right to tell you what I feel. I know, too, that if all things were equal, I could make you very much happier than the youngest Ambassador in Europe could ever do."

"You must not tell me and I must not . . . listen," Atalanta said. "Perhaps I should . . . go."

She looked away from him, but made no effort to rise.

Then she gave a little gasp as Paul suddenly knelt down beside her and took both her hands in his.

"I love you, Atalanta," he said passionately. "I want to go on saying it over and over again. I love everything about you. The innocent untouched look on your face. The flicker of fear in your eyes because never before has a man made love to you. The sweetness of your lips, the way in which your fingers, because I am holding them, are fluttering like a frightened bird. *Je t'aime*—I love you."

Atalanta felt herself quiver at the tone in his voice and then with what was a little cry she said:

"Why could we not have met before? Now it is too late . . . can you not understand it is . . . too late?"

"What you really mean," he said, rising to his feet, "is that I am too poor. Your parents would not welcome an impoverished artist as a son-in-law, however much he might love you, however much you might love him. How can I compete with a Viscount and an Ambassador?"

"It is not that. Papa and Mama are not snobs," Atalanta said hotly. "It is not only that William is a Viscount. It is because one day he will be the Earl of Winchcombe and I shall live in the house that was Mama's home."

She thought for a moment, then went on:

"I shall be important in our little world, the one in which I have been brought up. Can you understand that means more than anything to Mama? She does not exactly put it into words, but I know what she feels. It will be a triumph for her that I shall own the home from which she ran away. It is as if it were a justification of all she gave up in loving Papa."

"The trouble with you, Atalanta," Paul said slowly, "is that you are too clever. Why can you not be an ordinary stupid little girl with a lovely face? Then I should know that your position in Vallon would compensate you for everything else you will miss."

"Why will it not . . . do that?" Atalanta asked almost defiantly.

"Because you are sensitive and intuitive. Because you can understand what I am trying to say in my painting. Can you not see you will be hurt more violently and more profoundly than someone who is not so vulnerable, not attuned to all the real things that matter."

Atalanta did not answer and he went on:

"You are beautiful; you appreciate and understand beauty. Can you live with ugliness and not find it destroys you? The ugliness of sheer materialism, the ugliness of being unappreciated, of being touched by a man you do not love?"

He saw Atalanta shiver and went on.

"I cannot believe, Atalanta, that you will not long for something more, something spiritual, something of the soul which has nothing to do with the position into which you have married, but only concerns your heart."

"Stop saying all these . . . things to me!" Atalanta cried. "I cannot . . . listen to them! You know I . . . cannot."

She gave a little sob.

"Am I hurting you?" Paul asked. "If you are suffering a little, Atalanta, just think of what you are doing to me!"

"Do you really . . . mean that you . . . love me?" she asked. "It is . . . impossible!"

"Why is it?" he enquired. "I told you I did not believe in love at first sight, but from the moment I saw you I loved you. I love you, so overwhelmingly, so completely, that I know that for your own sake I must try and save you."

"How do you know I wish to be saved?" Atalanta asked.

She had risen as she spoke as if to leave him, and now she felt his hands on her shoulders as he turned her round to face him.

"Look at me, Atalanta," he said, "and do not lie."

"Why should I lie?" she enquired.

"Because you are trying to run away from yourself," he answered. "Answer me. Did you think of me last night?"

"Yes."

It was impossible, Atalanta thought, to tell him anything but the truth as he looked down at her, his eyes seeming to search deep into her soul.

"And if your cousin had not been waiting for you when you arrived home yesterday evening, would you not have run to me today? Wanting to hear what I had to say to you—wanting to know that I loved you?"

Atalanta was silent and he gave her shoulders a little shake.

"Answer me, Atalanta."

"I . . . can . . . not," she answered. "You have no . . . right to . . . question me. Let me . . . go!"

She tried to free herself, but he held her firmly.

"There is one other question, Atalanta, one very important one."

"What is . . . it?" she asked.

"Did your cousin kiss you?" Paul enquired. "Did he kiss your lips?"

Atalanta wanted to refuse to answer, but there was something in the quietness of his voice and the manner in which he spoke which made it impossible.

"N-no," she faltered. "No one has ever k-kissed me like t-that.'"

They looked at each other for a long moment, and then very gently as though he held something precious that he was afraid of hurting, Paul put his arms around her and drew her close.

He felt her quiver and yet she did not struggle. He looked down at her face and then he kissed her.

It was a very gentle kiss and her lips were soft beneath his. Then his arms tightened and for one moment his lips became possessive, insistent, demanding, before, with a superhuman effort of self-control, he set her free.

She stood looking at him wide-eyed and then she whispered: "Oh, why . . . did you kiss . . . me?"

"Because I was meant to be the first man to do so," Paul replied.

"It was w-wrong of . . . you . . . how shall I now . . . be able to . . . forget you as I have to do?"

"Must you forget me?"

"We are going to Paris on Friday."

"So soon?"

"The Duc d'Abencom is escorting Aunt Louise, Clementine, and me. He is coming to the Castle tonight because Clementine is to marry Prince Alexander of Vallon. She is very excited about it."

Paul smiled and said cynically.

"The most beautiful girl in England!"

"Yes, that is true," Atalanta agreed. "It is a pity you cannot see her; you would then . . . no longer be in . . . love with me."

"Perhaps that is a good idea," Paul said. "Can you not show me this paragon of beauty? It would solve every problem, would it not, Atalanta, if I no longer loved you?"

"There is no . . . problem as far as . . . I am . . . concerned," Atalanta managed to say.

"Do you really believe that?" he enquired. "Will you really be able to go to Paris and forget me so easily? Forget that I have kissed you! Forget the only kiss you have ever known?"

Atalanta clenched her hands until the knuckles were white.

"You shall see Clementine!" she whispered. "I do not believe that you can . . . love me so . . . suddenly. You are making me feel guilty and . . . unhappy and . . . I am sure it is just the sort of . . . illusion that you . . . Impressionists paint so . . . skillfully."

"How can I see her?" Paul asked.

"I am going back to the Castle tonight," Atalanta answered. "I shall look at the dinner party from the Minstrel's Gallery. Cicely has begged me to do so because she cannot see it herself. She hopes that Aunt Louise or Clementine will take the Duc to visit her, but sometimes they do not wish to explain to strangers about her accident. As the Duc is staying such a short time, there is every likelihood that she will not meet him, so I have promised to go back."

Atalanta looked up at Paul and went on.

"It is something I have done before because it keeps Cicely amused. Nobody will know I am there. The whole household will be busy helping with the dinner party. There are to be thirty guests and when there are so many everyone in the house has to give a hand downstairs."

"Are you suggesting that I should come with you?" Paul asked.

"Why not?" Atalanta said. "You wish to see Clementine. You shall see how beautiful she is and all the illusions you have about me will disappear."

"Are you prepared to gamble on it?" he enquired.

"With what stakes?" Atalanta asked bitterly. "I own nothing at the moment except some dilapidated old clothes of Clementine's. Of course you can trust me to pay my debt after I receive some of the Marriage Settlement Papa is negotiating with my uncle."

Atalanta stopped speaking and then she gave a little cry as Paul put his hands once again on her shoulders and shook her.

"Stop!" he said. "You are not to speak like that! It spoils you, Atalanta. You are reacting already to the harshness of this marriage you are making only for gain, which you are making against every decent instinct in your body. It is spoiling you, it is making you hard, worldly and cynical."

"No, please, it is not like that," Atalanta said unhappily, "please forgive me!"

She looked so beautiful when she was contrite, her eyes misty with unshed tears, that it was surprising that Paul did not take her again into his arms.

Instead, he said almost sternly: "Be yourself! Be the sweet, gentle little Goddess who came to me yesterday, looking at the world with surprised, innocent eyes, finding the simple things beautiful, believing in goodness because she is good herself."

He took his hands from her shoulders and, turning towards his easel, he said: "Come and sit down. We have to work. You are leaving for Paris on Friday and there is a great deal I must do to this picture before I lose you."

He spoke in a matter-of-fact voice and it seemed to Atalanta to bring their relationship to each other back to a kind of normality.

She was no longer agitated, no longer fighting against him, and she felt as if all the things he had said to her had been said in a dream.

"Can he really love me?" she asked herself, "and yet sit down at his easel, pick up his palette, and his brush and look at me as if I am no more than a model?"

Almost automatically she seated herself in the same position she had assumed the day before and linked her fingers together in her lap. She could see his profile, his features etched against the dark trunk of a tree.

He was so incredibly handsome and she knew that many women must have loved him. Had he told all of them that he had fallen in love at first sight?

She could still feel his lips against hers and her heart was still beating quicker because a man's mouth had touched her. Something within herself had quivered and come alive. She had hardly realised what it was.

She had only known, although she had never been kissed before, that Paul had treated her almost as if she were something sacred rather than a woman he desired.

"He was thinking of me rather than himself," she thought, yet her feelings were chaotic.

She had not expected him to say that he loved her, and yet she had told herself during the night that she knew that they both meant something to each other which could not have been put into words in any other way.

That moment of magic when they had looked at each other had locked them together.

"I must not think about it," she told herself. "I am going to Paris as William's intended wife."

Yet because she could not help herself she had to ask: "When will you be in Paris?"

"So you do want to see me again?" he said softly.

"Perhaps it will be . . . impossible to see you," Atalanta said.

"Nothing is impossible," he answered, "not if you want it enough."

"I must . . . go," Atalanta said, her voice quivering a little. "Mama will be expecting me and there is so much to do. Aunt Louise has sent a lot of Clementine's clothes to the Vicarage. She is also buying me three gowns from London and more when we get to Paris."

"Chains and shackles!" Paul said, without looking at her. "Very soon, Atalanta, the door of the prison will close and there will be no escape."

"I cannot escape. I must not even want to do so," Atalanta replied.

"When you are in Paris," Paul said, "I will show you my Studio."

"I would like that!" Atalanta cried. "I want to see the other pictures that you have done. Is your Studio in Montmartre?"

He nodded.

"Then somehow we must contrive for you to take me there," Atalanta said.

"Do you suppose that would be conduct becoming to the future wife of an Ambassador?" Paul asked mockingly.

She looked at him uncertainly.

"I will not tease you," he added, "and I will take you to my Studio simply so that you can see how a poor artist lives and be thankful you have escaped such squalor."

"You are not to talk like that!" Atalanta exclaimed. "You know it is not the squalor that I would mind or the poverty, or living in a Studio. It is just—"

"Papa, Mama, Bernard, Chryseis, and Hebe," Paul said. "You will learn, Atalanta, that invisible chains are much the most tenacious."

He rose to his feet as he spoke and put his palette down on the stool on which he had been sitting.

"It is only a sketch," he said, looking at the picture. "When I get back to Paris I am going to do a large picture of you and when it is finished I shall keep it to remind me that once a small Goddess took me almost to the top of Olympus, then left me alone and desolate."

"No, please . . ." Atalanta began.

She stopped what she was saying. Paul looked at her with a quizzical expression in his eyes.

"Will you not finish that sentence?" he suggested.

She shook her head.

"It is no . . . use," she answered. "I do not want you to be . . . hurt and yet there is nothing I can say to . . . prevent you feeling as you do."

"*Ma pauvre petite,*" he said, "it is hard to be torn between your very sensible, matter-of-fact brain and your warm, sensitive heart. One day we shall find out which is the stronger, but until then smile as you smiled at me yesterday. I am missing your dimples, I am missing the light in your eyes which made me feel happier than I have felt for many, many years."

"You have been unhappy?" Atalanta asked quickly.

"Very unhappy at times," he answered, "but I had grown philosophical. I had taught myself not to expect more than life was ready to give me—until yesterday. Then I became a fiery rebel ready to blow up the whole world if I can not get what I want."

There was a throb in his voice which made her move a few steps away from him.

"I must go," she said. "Will you come with me to-night, I want you to see Clementine and I know how thrilled Cicely will be to meet you. I told her about you today and she was very curious."

"You are quite certain I will not get you into trouble?" Paul asked.

"We should be very unlucky if anyone sees us," Atalanta answered. "No one will know that we have even been in the Castle if we are careful."

"Then where shall I meet you?" he asked.

"Here, at half after eight," Atalanta answered. "At

home we dine early and I often slip out to see to the animals. If I tell Mama later I have been to see Cicely, she will not be surprised."

"Very well," Paul said, "and thank you, Atalanta, for trusting me."

"Trusting me?" she asked in surprise.

"To be alone with you in the darkness," he answered. "I hope it is a privilege you do not accord to many men."

"But of course not," she answered. "No one has ever been to the Castle with me before."

"Again I am the first," Paul said softly and put out his hand.

Without thinking, Atalanta gave him her left hand and then, as he looked down at the engagement ring, she would have withdrawn it had he not held her fingers tightly in his.

"Your emerald is very magnificent and valuable," he said quizzically, "and in keeping with the position you will occupy, but not right for you. Emeralds are too hard and cold for Persephone."

"My Nurse always used to quote—Green and white, forsaken quite!" Atalanta said, trying to speak lightly. "I have felt superstitious about emeralds ever since."

"I think really you should wear diamonds," Paul said quietly as if he spoke to himself, "not huge overpowering gems, but small ones set like flowers which would sparkle like dewdrops in your hair or encircle your throat like a band of stardust."

It was when he was poetical that Atalanta thought it was hardest to resist him.

"I must . . . go," she murmured.

She had the feeling that he might take her in his arms again, and because she half-hoped that he would, and was frightened that he might, she turned and began to run away.

"Be here at half after eight," she cried over her shoulder, and once again he watched her move between the tree trunks until she was out of sight.

It was actually nearly nine o'clock before Atalanta appeared again, wending her way between the trees by the last light of the dying sun.

She found Paul waiting for her beside the path, leaning against a tree trunk.

"I am sorry if I am late," Atalanta said breathlessly. "But there was so much to do before dinner and when we had finished Mama made me try on some of the dresses she is going to alter."

"I thought perhaps you had forgotten me," Paul said.

"You know I would not do that," Atalanta replied. "Come, we follow the path across the park and enter the Castle by a side door. I have the key."

They walked quickly and spoke very little and yet it seemed to Atalanta that they were very close as they moved together under the branches of the great oak trees.

There was the caw-caw of the rooks going to roost, the coo of the wood pigeons, the hoot of a night owl, and the rustle of rabbits and small animals moving away from them in the grass.

Paul reached out and took her hand and it seemed to Atalanta that he too felt enchanted by the quiet of the evening. There was something almost mystical about it.

As they approached the Castle with its gaunt and majestic walls, Atalanta felt they were taking part in an adventure.

She opened a heavy-hinged oak door and they walked a long way along a dark passage and then up a very narrow stone staircase which led them to the first floor.

"This part of the Castle is uninhabited," she said in a low voice.

They passed through a baize door to find themselves in a thickly carpeted and lighted corridor. Atalanta led the way to Cicely's bedroom.

"Wait here a moment," she said to Paul and entered the room to find, as she had expected, that Cicely was alone.

"Atalanta!" Cicely exclaimed. "I thought you would come! I felt you would not be able to resist the chance of seeing the Duc."

"Have you met him?" Atalanta asked.

"No," Cicely replied. "Mama came in before dinner to tell me how gracious and charming he is. They are all bowled over by him!"

"I have brought someone to see you," Atalanta said.

"Not the artist!" Cicely enjaculated.

"He wanted to see the dinner party, so I will take him with me to the Minstrel's Gallery."

"I must see him! Bring him here quickly!" Cicely cried. "How sweet of you, Atalanta! It is the most exciting thing that has ever happened to me."

Atalanta smiled and opened the door for Paul. He walked to the side of the bed, and taking Cicely's hand in his, he raised it to his lips.

"A Sleeping Princess in a medieval Castle!" he exclaimed. "What more could an artist ask?"

Cicely laughed in delight.

"You are just as exciting as Atalanta said you were."

"I hoped Atalanta had said nice things about me."

"She has and I have so much wanted to meet you," Cicely replied.

"Well, I am here," Paul said, "and Atalanta wants me to see your sister, who she tells me is the most beautiful girl in England."

"She is lovely," Cicely said, "but not as nice as Atalanta."

"I agree with you," Paul answered. "No one could be as wonderful as Atalanta, or as interesting as you."

Cicely looked up at him, her eyes alight.

"Do you say flattering things like that to every woman you meet?" she asked.

"Only when I find them irrestitibly attractive," Paul replied, smiling.

"We had better go now to the Minstrel's Gallery," Atalanta said quickly. "Nurse may come back to see how

Cicely is, and I should get into terrible trouble with
Aunt Louise if she knew I had brought Paul here."

"Nurse will be too busy eating titbits in the pantry,"
Cicely said. "But you had better hurry to the Minstrel's Gallery. They will have almost reached the last
course by now."

"I hope we shall meet again, Lady Cicely," Paul said.
"I think you are very brave, and I am sure that one
day you will be downstairs at the Banquet, instead of
having to lie up here alone."

"Thank you," Cicely replied. "You have made me feel
much better about it and I do long to be downstairs."

"You will be," Paul said, and there was something
prophetic in his tone.

He kissed her hand, then followed Atalanta into the
corridor. Halfway down it, she opened a small door in
the paneling and he saw a set of very narrow steps.

"Do not make a sound," Atalanta whispered and
slipped off her shoes.

Paul did likewise and they moved forward in stock-
inged feet. They had to feel their way as there was only
little light ahead of them.

The stairs were quite short and they led into a very
small room set above the Dining Hall. It was furnished
only with a piano and the chairs used by the musicians
when they played for a dance.

It was easy to see the guests below.

A huge table stretched the whole length of the Hall
and was decorated with gold and silver ornaments and
china bowls of hothouse peaches and purple grapes, all
intertwined with flowers which encircled the ornaments
and the huge light-candle candelabra with which the
table was lit.

At the far end of the table, facing the gallery, the
Countess was wearing a glittering tiara of sapphires
and diamonds almost like a crown on her head.

On her right was the Duc d'Abencom and beside him
Clementine.

The Duc was a handsome man, dark-haired with a

small imperial beard and seemingly amused and entertained by the party which had been given in his honour.

He was laughing and using his hands to illustrate what he was saying, and Clementine, who was smiling, was looking her very best.

Her hair, deep gold in the light of the candelabra, seemed to halo her face with its classic features and her eyes, which were often cold and unresponsive, seemed now, because she was amused, bright and shining.

Atalanta saw Paul watching her and felt a sudden pang of jealousy.

"She is lovely," she told herself, "far lovelier than I could ever be, and now he will see how foolish he has been to imagine that he could fall in love with me. Because he is a foreigner, he is attracted by fair-haired, blue-eyed women, and because he is a foreigner he can say things which make my heart turn over in my breast and give me that strange feeling of excitement so that it is difficult to breathe. But they mean nothing and I am being stupid—very stupid to take him seriously."

She looked down below and thought that perhaps at the next party that was given at the Castle, she would be sitting at the table as William's wife—a Viscountess —on equal terms with the other ladies of the County.

Then Atalanta could only think of how Paul had held her in his arms and kissed her for the first time. And the candelabra, silver dishes, glittering jewels—all seemed to swim in front of her eyes.

Would she feel the same when William kissed her, her brain asked? She had no desire to face the question.

Paul was still watching the guests below and she touched his arm.

"We must go," she said.

He turned towards her instantly and followed her up the narrow staircase until she opened the door at the top, which led them out into the deserted corridor.

They slipped on their shoes, and without speaking Atalanta led the way through the baize door and back through the empty uninhabited part of the Castle.

By now, it was very dark and she realised that, while she knew her way, Paul had reached out to touch the wall.

She slipped her hand into his.

"It is quite straightforward. We walk straight ahead until we reach the staircase."

"I will follow where you lead," he answered.

She held him by the hand until they reached the staircase.

"Hold on to the banisters," she said, and he followed her until they came to the door that led out onto the park.

She locked it behind them. In the soft purple dusk, it was still possible to see their way, but nevertheless she did not protest when Paul took her hand.

They walked for some moments in silence until Atalanta said: "You do see how beautiful she is?"

"Who? Lady Clementine?" he enquired. "Very pretty! Exactly how an English girl should look."

There was something dry about his words which made Atalanta say: "Surely you are not being critical?"

"Why should I?" he enquired. "I admire her very much as a type, but I have no desire to paint her."

Atalanta could not help feeling a sudden warmth creep into her heart.

"You have not fallen in love with her?"

She managed to speak lightly, although she knew the question was significant.

"I have fallen in love only once in my life," Paul answered. "I am not pretending to you, Atalanta, that there have not been many women who have attracted me, who I thought at the time were utterly and completely desirable, but I know now I was never really in love."

Atalanta did not speak and he went on: "It is

71

strange how it happens so suddenly, and yet so completely, that there is no argument about it."

"Perhaps one could fall out of love just as quickly," Atalanta said in a very small voice.

"I think you know in your heart that that is not true," Paul said. "When something really fundamental, really important happens, it sweeps away all that is tawdry, all that is unessential. Surely you with your perception can understand that."

"I still doubt that you are . . . really in . . . love with . . . me," Atalanta said.

It was easy to talk, she thought, because she could not see Paul's face and he could not see hers.

"Then I shall have to prove it to you," Paul said.

"How can you do that if we do not see each other?" Atalanta asked.

"But we will," he answered. "You see, Little Atalanta, it is not going to be very easy for you to lose me, and I shall not give up hope of winning you until the wedding ring is actually on your finger."

"But I must not let you hope for something which is impossible," Atalanta said quickly. "If we had met in other circumstances, or before yesterday, it might have been different. Not now it is too late! We have to forget each other; you must see that."

"You may feel you have to forget me," Paul said, "but I could not forget you, Atalanta, even if I tried. And because I am a determined sort of man, because when I want something I strive in every way possible to get it, I have no intention of giving up so easily."

"What do you mean?" Atalanta said.

"Is it not quite obvious?" he said. "I am going to try to make you love me. In fact if the truth were known, I think you do love me a little, even if you will not admit it."

"No . . . that is not . . . true!" Atalanta cried.

"Is it not?" Paul enquired. "Tell me, Atalanta, if I had told you tonight that I thought your Cousin, Clementine, was the most beautiful, wonderful person I had ever seen in my life, would you not have been a little disappointed?"

Atalanta did not answer and he laughed.

"Oh, darling, you are so young and so completely and utterly transparent! I knew what you were feeling—I think I will always know what you are feeling—as we peeped through the Minstrel's Gallery at Lady Clementine. You would not admit it to me, but I know you were at that moment just a tiny bit apprehensive, and perhaps a little bit jealous, that I might find her more attractive than you."

There was nothing Atalanta could say, and now he slipped his arm through hers as they walked up the path which led into the wood.

As they reached the first of the pine trees, he stopped and put his arms round her.

"I am going to say good-bye to you now, Atalanta. Tomorrow you will be too busy and on Friday you go to Paris. I shall find you there. There is much I want to show you."

"I do not even know where I am staying," Atalanta said desperately. "I forgot to ask Aunt Louise, and if I do not see you tomorrow how can I tell you where I shall be?"

"I am quite certain you will be at the British Embassy and, if you are not, I will find out where you are. Do not worry. Just be ready to slip away when you can and let me show you a very different side of Paris from what you will see in the august company of Ambassadors and Royal Princes."

Atalanta was acutely conscious of his arms round her and his face very near to hers.

It was difficult in the darkness of the trees to remember that she should not let him touch her. She knew she should hurry home and not listen to what he was saying to her. But it was impossible to move.

"Good-bye, little Goddess," Paul said gently, "or rather *au revoir*. We shall not lose each other, and while we are apart will you remember that I am thinking of you, longing for you, loving you, every moment of the day and the night?"

He bent his head as he spoke and found her lips.

She knew it was wrong, she knew she should not let him, but her will had gone. She could no longer think; she could only feel.

She felt his mouth, warm and possessive against hers, and then that strange flicker of fire which she had known earlier in the day rose again within herself and became more intense, more exciting every moment.

She felt herself tremble and thrill as she had never done before, until even as she wanted him to hold her even closer, to kiss her and to go on kissing her, he had set her free.

"I love you," Paul said very quietly. "Never forget that I love you."

Because she knew he expected it of her, Atalanta moved away from him.

She hardly realised where she was going or why she must leave him. She just knew that something unbelievably wonderful had come to an end and there was nothing more to be said.

She reached the end of the wood as if in a dream.

Then she was running wildly, almost frantically, down the dusty road toward the Vicarage.

Chapter Four

ALL the way to Paris, Atalanta was rebuked by her conscience.

"How could I have behaved in such an immodest manner?" she asked herself over and over again as she remembered how she had let Paul kiss her and how her lips had responded to his when they said good-bye.

She was aware that something quite unaccountable had happened when she had felt his arms round her and his mouth had found hers.

It had been different the first time he kissed her.

That had been disturbing enough, but she had not then experienced emotions as overpowering as when he held her close to him in the darkness of the wood, and she had found it impossible not to respond to the excitement she knew she had aroused in him.

"I must have been mad," she said to herself, and she kept wondering if he had been shocked and perhaps disgusted by her behaviour.

"Would any real lady," she asked herself, "have behaved in such a way?"

It seemed to Atalanta that from the moment she had met Paul she had become another person.

Never before had she wanted so desperately to see a man. Never before had she longed for the moment when she would be close to him and would hear his voice.

The fact that they had talked together and that she had allowed him to pay her compliments was bad enough.

But to allow him to embrace her without protest, to have known that strange feeling of breathlessness when he looked down into her eyes, and to have felt a flame flicker within her body was something which, she told herself, was inexcusable.

Yet she now wanted more than she had ever wanted anything in her life before to see him again.

"He has gone, our association, such as it was, is finished," she thought. "He may have returned to Paris, but he does not even know my address."

She told herself these things, and yet she could only remember Paul saying that they would meet again and that he would find her wherever she might be staying.

And she knew, reprehensible though it might be, that she would give up her hope of Heaven for a chance of hearing his voice again and being conscious of his eyes looking down into hers.

She had risen very early in the morning and walked to the Castle to see Cicely.

At least that is what she told herself she was doing, but if she was honest she knew she hoped to find Paul in the wood.

It was almost like a blow to find he was not there. She had hoped against all common sense, against the fact that he had said good-bye, that she would find him sitting at his easel as she came down the path which led to the Castle.

The talk about him to Cicely was some compensation.

"He is charming and so handsome!" Cicely exclaimed. "How could you be so clever as to find anyone so exciting in the woods? It is just like a fairy story!"

"I came back to tell you about the Duc," Atalanta said.

"I am not interested in the Duc," Cicely retorted, "and besides Mama talks about him all the time. Tell me more about Paul Beaulieu."

"He has gone back to Paris," Atalanta said, hearing the note of despair in her voice.

"Then you will see him when you get there," Cicely suggested.

"I think it is unlikely," Atalanta replied. "I could not even tell him where we are staying."

"At the British Embassy of course," Cicely said. "William has arranged everything. You will be very grand and they will make a tremendous fuss of you. At least that is what Mama expects."

Atalanta felt her spirits lift a little. Paul would at least be able to find her there—if he wished to do so.

There was very little more she could say to Cicely and every question that the girl asked made her feel more guilty.

She had let Paul kiss her, not once, but twice, and she knew nothing about him. There never seemed to be time to ask him about himself.

Who were his family? Where had he lived before he went to Paris? All she knew was that he was an Impressionist painter and he had a studio in Montmartre.

"What does it matter?" Atalanta thought with a shrug of her shoulders. "All I care about is whether he will want to see me again."

In the train and on the boat Atalanta found it difficult to be interested in her surroundings.

On any other occasion she would have been wild with delight at the thought of traveling abroad, of crossing the Channel and seeing France.

But now she could only feel Paul's arms around her,

and know that her heart fluttered in her breast as she remembered the touch of his lips.

"You are very quiet, Atalanta," the Countess said sharply. "I hope you are feeling well. I have no desire to arrive in Paris with a sick girl on my hands!"

"I am quite well, thank you, Aunt Louise," Atalanta replied.

"I must say that is a very smart traveling outfit," the Countess said. "Your bonnet will refute the French caricatures which hold us up to ridicule as the dowdy English."

The Countess had already remarked on Atalanta's clothes before, and her niece was well aware that there was a note of resentment in her voice because the blue dress, with its pelisse to match, made her look so attractive.

There was, as the Countess had pointed out on innumerable occasions, no suggestion that there should be any comparison between her and Clementine.

But at the same time, where "the most beautiful girl in England" was concerned, the entourage surrounding her should preferably be as drab and unobtrusive as possible.

Because Clementine was in good spirits and excited about meeting the Prince, she looked her very best, and when finally they arrived in Paris late in the evening, Atalanta saw the expressions of admiration on the faces of the Embassy Officials who had accompanied William to the station.

William came aboard the train as soon as it drew into the Gare du Nord, and the Countess waited for him in their compartment so that he could greet them privately.

"It is delightful to see you, Mama," he said. "I hope the journey passed comfortably."

"The Duc looked after us most admirably," the Countess replied. "He is in the next compartment, as he wished to smoke."

"An Aide-de-camp from his own Embassy will attend to him," William said. "How are you, Atalanta?"

He spoke to Atalanta casually, and as he made no movement either to take her hand or to kiss her cheek, Clementine moved forward to embrace her brother.

"I cannot tell you, dear William, how excited I am," she said. "The Duc has been charming. You must thank him for making our journey such a pleasant one."

His Grace had in fact, Atalanta thought, seen to it that they were treated like Royalty from the moment they left England.

Two *Cabines de Luxe* were reserved for them on the steamer, two private compartments on the train, and the Duc's valet and a Courier, who had accompanied him to England, saw to the baggage and arranged for all possible comforts, such as refreshments, footwarmers, and rugs, to be at their disposal.

Atalanta had hardly spoken to the Duc because he was so busy entertaining the Countess and Clementine, but he had the tact not to inflict his company upon them for long, knowing there was nothing more fatiguing than having to converse while traveling.

Atalanta saw William's eyes flicker over her new gown and elegant bonnet. She felt that he approved.

"There are two carriages here from the Embassy," he said to his Mother, "and of course the baggage will go with the servants."

"I hope you have managed to engage another Lady's maid," the Countess said. "I can see that Martha will have little time for the girls if she is to look after me properly."

"Everything has been seen to by the Housekeeper at the Embassy," William replied. "I assure you, Mama, you will be very comfortable and Lord Lyons, our Ambassador, is looking forward to entertaining you."

When they left the train, the Station Master, resplendent in a gold-braided uniform, escorted them to their carriage. The Countess and William were to travel in one, and as the carriages were rather small the two girls were accommodated in another.

"They will be only just behind us," William said as his mother demurred. "There is really not room in these town vehicles for four people."

"And what about the Duc?" Clementine asked.

"His Grace will have his own carriage to meet him," William replied.

At that moment, the Duc came up to them.

"I must bid you *au revoir, Madame,* and thank you for your most kind and generous hospitality," he said to the Countess. "I will be calling on you tomorrow to make an appointment for you to meet His Royal Highness. Until then I know I leave you in good hands."

"We are most grateful to Your Grace for looking after us so ably," the Countess said graciously.

The Duc bowed to Clementine.

"*Au revoir, Mademoiselle.*"

"I hope we shall see you tomorrow," Clementine said in a low voice.

"You can be sure of it," the Duc answered.

He held her hand closely in his and it seemed to Atalanta that he held it a little longer than was strictly necessary.

Then he bowed to Atalanta and moved away as the ladies stepped into the carriages.

They were quite small barouches, well padded and with elegant silver accoutrements bearing the British Coat-of-Arms. The coachman and footman were both splendidly attired in distinctive livery.

Clementine sank back against the cushions with a little sigh.

"He is charming, quite charming!" she exclaimed.

"The Duc?" Atalanta questioned.

"He has such an air of distinction," Clementine went on, "even if one had no idea who he was, one would know he was an aristocrat!"

"What did he tell you about the Prince?" Atalanta enquired.

"He said most flattering things about him," Clementine answered, "but that was, after all, what he was sent to England to do."

"How do you feel about marrying a man whom you have never seen?" Atalanta asked.

"Why should it matter?" Clementine replied. "After all, *mariages de convenance* are always arranged amongst Royal Families as they are amongst the aristocrats in France."

"Suppose you both hate each other when you meet?" Atalanta asked.

"I think you are being very bourgeois," Clementine said crushingly. "Amongst educated, civilised people there is no possibility of such a vulgar emotion."

"No, of course not," Atalanta agreed.

She was not really interested in what Clementine was saying because she was bending forward to have her first glimpse of Paris.

There were gas lights flaring in their white oval-shaped globes, interspersed between tall leafy plane trees in a broad street, which Atalanta realised must be one of Baron Haussmann's new Boulevards.

Through the open window came a noise she had never heard before.

It was the sound of fiacres and three-horse buses combined with the chattering voices of the crowds on the Café terraces. She could see street vendors moving amongst them crying their wares.

There was the sudden music from a grinding barrel organ, and it seemed to Atalanta that she could also hear the ceaseless tread of feet as the crowds moved up and down the pavements talking, laughing, shouting.

She had not believed that people could seem so gay, so full of life and laughter.

She bent forward a little further. The traffic in itself was fascinating. There were black-and-yellow fiacres with their blinds down, dashing along at a pace which appeared almost dangerous amongst the slower traffic, the *cochers* in tophats and cape-coats, with imperious disregard of the needs of the fashionable landaus or the slower calèches clopping along sedately with their candle lanterns already lit.

There were shops blazing with light and crowded with customers, although it was very late.

At the Café's tables spread out on the pavement, Atalanta could see men with dark beards and enormous mustaches under glistening tophats.

Women with long trailing skirts swept by, while under the gas lamps stood other women, red-lipped, dark-eyed, in low-necked dresses, who smiled invitingly.

"This is Paris, Clementine!" Atalanta cried. "Paris! And how exciting it is!"

"I am not interested in all these common people," Clementine said. "The Ambassador will be giving parties for us and then we shall meet the elite."

"I want to see the real Paris," Atalanta replied. "I would like to sit at a Café and watch the people passing by."

"You should not say anything like that to Mama, or she will certainly send you home immediately!" Clementine answered. "I hope you are going to behave properly, Atalanta. After all, you should remember that in the position I shall hold shortly I shall be Royal."

"Of course I will not forget that," Atalanta promised.

"Then behave in a circumspect manner," Clementine said sharply. "William said you had a lot to learn and I am sure he is right. Indeed, what could you know of society living as you have in Little Combe?"

Atalanta gave a sigh. Once again her relations from the Castle were doing their best to make her feel awkward and unimportant.

That was the way Aunt Louise had always treated Mama, and Clementine, Atalanta decided, was very like her.

There was no point in arguing. She should really be very grateful to her Aunt for the clothes she had been given from London, and some of Clementine's gowns which had been sent to the Vicarage were actually almost new, so Mama had managed to alter them quite skillfully.

Atalanta felt guilty when she thought of these gowns.

She knew when she had walked up to the Castle early on Friday morning that she was neglecting her duty in not settling down immediately after breakfast to sew up the hems of Clementine's old dresses and take them in at the waist.

But when she got back to the Vicarage, it was to find that Lady Evelyn had organized a whole working party.

There were three women from the village who were good sewers, and Miss Makins, the retired governess who taught the twins, all stitching away.

"You still need at least two afternoon dresses and several more evening gowns if you are to go to many parties," Lady Evelyn said. "I know that as William's future wife you will feel sadly unfashionable if you wear the same gown over and over again."

"Perhaps you better tell Aunt Louise that," Atalanta suggested. "She will merely think I am being greedy or grasping."

"Oh, darling, how wonderful it will be when you have money of your own and do not have to rely on their charity!" Lady Evelyn exclaimed.

"I know, Mama. It is galling to think that we have to depend on them for every penny. And they do not let us forget how grateful we should be."

Lady Evelyn gave a little sigh, but said no more, and Atalanta knew how much she disliked having to write the letter of almost groveling thanks to her sister-in-law for the three dresses Atalanta had received from London.

A great consolation was that they were very pretty.

Atalanta told herself that no one would think she was as poor as a church mouse when she appeared in the white gown with its train of tulle frills swept round at the back with a blue sash ending with a huge bow, or the afternoon dress of pale-blue batiste with its tiny touches of lace and little pearl buttons from the neck to the waist.

The carriage had left the Boulevard now and turned into a narrower street. Atalanta saw the name written up as they turned the corner and gave a little cry of excitement.

"We are there, Clementine! This is the Rue du Faubourg St. Honoré and in a moment we shall be at the British Embassy."

She did not know quite what she had expected, but when they turned in through the huge gates, which gave entrance from the street into a large courtyard, Atalanta had her first sight of the eighteenth-century house which had once belonged to the Princess Pauline Bonaparte, sister of Napoleon.

It was very impressive and very beautiful.

When they alighted from the carriages to join William and the Countess at the top of the red-carpeted steps, flunkeys with powdered wigs and gold-emblazoned livery led them into the large entrance hall, through an Ante-Room and into the *Salon d'Honneur*.

It was an enormous room with gilded Ionic columns, and here Lord Lyons, the English Ambassador, came forward to greet them.

"My Mother—My Lord," William said. "My sister and my fiancée, Atalanta Lynton."

Atalanta sank down in a deep curtsy. The Ambassador, whom she saw was old but very distinguished, said: "It is delightful to see you, Lady Winchcombe, I hope you have had a good journey and that the sea was not rough."

"No, indeed, it was quite calm and fortunately we are all good travellers," the Countess answered.

"I am glad to hear it," the Ambassador replied. "Personally I only leave Paris once a year when I go to London, and I always dread these occasions. Now I am getting old I prefer to spend my time inside the Embassy gates and let the world come to me."

He led the party from the *Salon d'Honneur* into one of the most beautiful rooms Atalanta had ever seen. It was in the centre of the house and, as she was to learn the next day, it looked down the whole length of the garden.

Decorated in white and gold with enormous chandeliers it was lit by candles, and almost involuntarily she exclaimed aloud: "How beautiful!"

The Ambassador turned to her with a smile.

"I am glad you think so, Miss Lynton. This was the private Drawing Room of the Princess Pauline. It is known as the *Salon Blanc et Or* and it is here that she received her friends. I expect William has told you the history of this house?"

Seeing Atalanta's interest, the Ambassador continued. "It was bought by the Duke of Wellington in 1814 when we had defeated the French and the Princess Pauline was desperately in need of money. It was the first Embassy to be owned by the British Government and we are very proud of it."

"I am not surprised," Atalanta said with obvious sincerity, and the Ambassador smiled at her.

As if the Countess resented Atalanta monopolising the Ambassador, she started to talk to him of the plans for their visit and Atalanta could learn no more about her surroundings, except to look around her.

Finally they were taken upstairs to the second floor, where their bedrooms were situated.

Atalanta's was the smallest room, at the very end of the house, and like the other rooms overlooked the garden.

"I'm afraid it is not a very large bedchamber, Miss Lynton," the English Housekeeper said apologetically, "but the Embassy is very overcrowded. There have been complaints since 1842 from the secretaries and Officials who have to work in the Gate House."

"Yet the building looks enormous!" Atalanta exclaimed.

"We have to fit guests in as if they were pieces of a puzzle," the Housekeeper replied. "Of course having running water, which His Lordship has installed this year, is a real help, but these old houses are always cold, and that's a fact!"

"That will not worry us this time of the year." Atalanta smiled.

"Lady Fitzalan—that's His Lordship's niece who acts as hostess for him—insists on a fire in the Schoolroom," the Housekeeper replied in a voice which showed this was a continual bone of contention.

"The Schoolroom?" Atalanta questioned.

"For Her Ladyship's two little daughters," the House-keeper explained. "Nice little ladies, but they occupy a bedroom apiece and there is another for Miss Dill, their governess, apart from the Schoolroom itself. No wonder we are overcrowded!"

The Housekeeper was a garrulous gossip and Atalanta was glad when she was alone.

It was now quite dark, and although she stood at the window she could see little save a glow in the distance which she guessed came from the gaslamps which lit the Champs Élysées leading up to the Arc de Triomphe.

She had asked her Father about Paris before she left home, but it was many years since he had been there and he said the City must have changed a good deal.

"I have not seen the alterations," he said, "the new Boulevards, the Champs Élysées, or the Place Vendome with its statue of Napoleon put up in 1806. You must write to me, Atalanta, and tell me everything you see. I went abroad a great deal as a young man and I would love to go again."

He spoke wistfully and Atalanta knew he was think-ing it was lack of money which prevented him, money which tied him to Little Combe from which he could escape only in his thoughts and in his imagination.

"I will write and describe everything as well as I can, Papa," Atalanta promised and kissed him impulsively.

"You are a good child, Atalanta," he said, "and be-cause you have an excellent brain you will see and enjoy far more than the average traveler. Try to understand the people of France—that is the secret of enjoying any country!"

"I will try, Papa," Atalanta answered, and knew that those she really wished to understand and learn about were called the Impressionists.

As they had arrived so late, supper was served in the Sitting Room on the first floor which had been allotted to the Countess and her party while they were staying at the Embassy.

William joined them, and, producing a list of their engagements, he started to explain to his Mother and to Clementine the people they would meet and the luncheons and dinners at which they would be entertained in the next few days.

"When shall I see the Prince?" Clementine asked.

"The Duc has, of course, first to make a report officially on his visit to Castle Combe," William replied. "Then the Prince will signify through the Duc when he will be pleased to receive you."

"Atalanta asked me while we were driving from the station what would happen if the Prince and I hated each other," Clementine said.

"Really, Atalanta, what a ridiculous question!" the Countess exclaimed sharply, while William, giving her what she felt was his coldest and most contemptuous glance, said: "I think Atalanta's questions on this matter need not concern us."

The subject was closed and only Atalanta felt a little resentful that Clementine had chosen to show her up in such bad light.

She knew quite well that such a question asked privately need not have been discussed or mentioned in front of her Aunt and especially William.

"As we came away in such a hurry," the Countess said, "Clementine and I need clothes. I thought we would visit Monsieur Worth tomorrow. I am sure we could persuade him to make up some gowns very quickly, especially if we tell him we shall require a wedding gown for Clementine."

William looked alarmed.

"You must not mention that Vallon is receiving its Independence until after the Treaty has been signed! Remember, Mama, that is very important! Everybody in the Embassy is aware of what is occurring and you can speak of it quite freely to the Ambassador, but we do not wish the Press to make any comment until the President and the Prince have actually affixed their signatures to the papers on which Sir Heatherington and I have been working for so long."

"Of course, I understand," the Countess said. "And now, William, after such a long and very exhausting journey I think we shall all retire to our rooms. The girls will be up early tomorrow to see the sights of Paris. I hope you have planned an itinerary."

"Yes, indeed," William answered, "but I think the Duc will be calling early in the morning and Clementine must receive him."

"Yes, of course," Clementine agreed.

"After that," William continued, "you will be free to go to the dressmakers, see Notre Dame or any of the other sights that will attract you."

"I hope you will accompany us," his mother suggested.

"I doubt if I shall have the time," William replied. "I am very busy, Mama, as you can imagine. But, however, there are various Aides-de-Camp in the Embassy and one of them will certainly accompany you wherever you wish to go."

"Then please arrange it," the Countess said. "Good night, dear boy."

She swept out of the room as she spoke like a ship in full sail. Clementine followed, while Atalanta waited for a moment, thinking perhaps William would wish to say something personal to her.

He stood, looking her up and down, and then with a faint smile he remarked: "Your gown is certainly an improvement on the last one I saw you wearing. I have told Mama that you are to be well dressed. Do not let her be so immersed in bedecking Clementine that you are forgotten."

"I am sorry that I cannot provide my own trousseau," Atalanta said, feeling suddenly very humble.

"I am well aware that is impossible," William remarked, "and of course you realise, Atalanta, that your appearance reflects on me."

"Yes, I am aware of that," Atalanta said in a low voice.

"And while we are speaking of it," William went on, "I see no reason for you to tell people too much about the manner in which you live when you are in England."

"You mean you do not wish them to know that my Father is the Vicar of Little Combe?" Atalanta asked.

"People are not really interested in what particular circumstances you have been brought up," William said. "You are my cousin, your Mother is my Father's sister; that is all they need to know."

"I am not ashamed of my family," Atalanta declared with a little spark of anger in her eyes.

"Your family are not of any consequence in Paris," William replied. "What is important is that my future wife should be of gentle birth, and that people should admire my choice. You are pretty, Atalanta, and you have great possibilities. But you need grooming, you need dressing, and you need the polish that only comes from moving in the very best society."

He paused, and added impressively, "I will do my best to instruct you in the behaviour to be expected of you, but you must be very careful not to make mistakes. Do not talk too much. Do not accept an invitation without consulting me first. Is that clear?"

"Yes, William, very clear," Atalanta agreed.

"I feel sure we shall manage to get along very well together when we know each other better," William said. "Tomorrow I shall introduce you to some of my friends; they are already extremely curious about you."

"Let us hope they will not be disappointed," Atalanta said sharply.

Then, feeling she could bear no more, she dropped him a little curtsy.

"Good night, William."

She had the feeling he was about to say something else, but she did not stop to hear what it was. She hurried away from the Sitting Room, found the staircase which led to the second floor, and went to her bedroom.

Clementine's bedroom was some way from hers. She passed the door, but she did not stop to say good night. She went into her own room and closed the door with a bang.

"Why," she asked her reflection in the mirror, "must William always speak as if I were a naughty schoolgirl!"

She saw the flash of anger in her eyes then, turning away from the mirror and unbuttoning her gown, she began to get ready for bed.

She was half-undressed when she went to the window, drew back the curtains, and leaned out.

The night was still and warm. She almost fancied she could hear the music and the noise of the Boulevards. She could smell the fragrance of flowers.

The air seemed lighter and more buoyant than it was in England, and Atalanta felt a wave of excitement creep over her.

She was in Paris and Paul was in Paris, too! She was sure he was thinking of her as she was thinking of him.

If only they could meet, if only they could go out together.

She felt like a bird in a golden cage, and she longed with a desperate, uncontrollable desire to escape and see him again.

The following day, Atalanta accompanied the Countess and Clementine shopping. They visited the famous mansion of Monsieur Worth.

The English genius had made the crinolines of the Empress Eugenie the envy of every fashionable woman in the world.

Now his dresses, caught back into a long train at the back with their frills and sashes, their tight bodices and lace-trimmed collars, were each more ravishing than the last.

The Countess ordered half-a-dozen gowns for herself, nearly a dozen for Clementine, and reluctantly, only because Clementine reminded her of William's instructions, two for Atalanta.

"If we had more time, I am sure we could find you something cheaper which would suit you just as well," the Countess said acidly to Atalanta as they left the shop.

"Perhaps I could try to find some less expensive shops when you and Clementine are busy," Atalanta suggested.

"Martha could go with you or maybe Clementine's maid, Jeanne," the Countess said. "She may even know of a little dressmaker who would run you up several gowns for a few francs."

"I will try and find out if she knows of one," Atalanta promised.

They had returned to the Embassy where a luncheon was being given by the Ambassador in honor of the Spanish Ambassador.

Clementine and the Countess were lunching with the Duc in the house that had previously been the Vallon Embassy, but Atalanta ate in the State Dining Room of which Queen Victoria had approved the decorations when she was in Paris in 1855.

After lunch the guests walked from the French windows into the garden and from there onto the lawns.

Beyond, there were thick shrubberies filled with flowering bushes and chestnut trees, their blossoms like pink-and-white candles.

There were several elderly diplomats at the party who paid Atalanta compliments and to whom she chattered away in her excellent French, finding them easy to talk to and discovering to her surprise that the meal was far less stiff than the functions which took place at Castle Combe.

Lady Fitzalan's little daughters were brought into the garden by their governess. They were pretty children dressed in crisp white-muslin gowns with pink sashes.

Atalanta saw the governess standing stiffly in the background and, feeling sorry for her, introduced herself.

"I am Atalanta Lynton," she said, holding out her hand.

Miss Dill curtsyed. She was a pretty young woman, not more than twenty-three with dark-brown hair primly arranged under a plain bonnet.

She had, however, exceptionally beautiful brown eyes and it seemed to Atalanta that she stared at her in a strange and rather searching manner.

"Do you like being in Paris?" Atalanta asked conventionally.

"It has been wonderful, more wonderful than I can ever say," Miss Dill replied impulsively.

Then to Atalanta's surprise, her expression changed and the light faded from her eyes.

It was as if she was suddenly stricken by her own thoughts. Then before Atalanta could speak, she moved hastily away to pick up a handkerchief dropped by one of the little girls.

Finally the guests began to depart and the Countess and Clementine returned from their party. One of the English Aides-de-camp suggested that they should visit the Louvre.

"I have some work to do," William said quickly, "but I am sure you, Mama, and the girls would enjoy the pictures. Captain Bruntwood is quite an authority on art, so he can tell you all about them."

Captain Bruntwood looked gratified at William's praise and hurried away to arrange for a carriage, while the Countess, Clementine, and Atalanta went upstairs to fetch their cloaks and put on their bonnets.

Atalanta was sitting in front of the mirror in her room when Marie, the young French maid whom she had learnt that morning had been allotted to look after her, came into the room and shut the door behind her.

"There is a note for you, M'selle," she said in French. "It came while you were at luncheon and I was told to give it to you when you were alone."

"A note for me?" Atalanta asked excitedly.

She held out her hand. The maid brought out a white envelope from beneath her white apron.

"The messenger who brought it said I was to give it into your hands and let no one else see me do it."

"Who was it?" Atalanta asked.

The maid shrugged her shoulders.

"Was he tall, dark, and good-looking?"

The maid shook her head and smiled.

"No, M'selle. He was small—an elderly man, a servant."

For a moment, Atalanta felt disappointed, then she realised that Paul would not have taken the risk of coming to the Embassy himself.

She opened the note as soon as the maid had left the room. It was short and she read quickly:

Ma Chére,

I cannot wait any longer. I expect that you will go to your room to lie down between five and seven o'clock. As soon as you can, cross the garden, keeping out of sight of the main rooms. Go through the shrubbery and you will find a door in the wall. Open it. There will be a sentry outside and I shall be in a closed carriage. I shall wait until seven o'clock. If you cannot come today, then I shall be there again tomorrow. You have been in my thoughts every second we have been apart. I cannot think or breathe or live without you. Your beauty haunts me.

Paul.

Atalanta read the letter through twice, then pressed it against her breast. Her first love letter!

She would see him! He was here in Paris; he was thinking of her as she had been thinking of him! But would she be able to get away?

She had no idea whether she would be expected to rest, but sure enough, when they returned from seeing the pictures in the Louvre, the Countess said:

"Dinner is at eight o'clock. We are dining here in the Embassy and going to a Reception afterwards. You girls are to lie down. Sleep so that you will look your best this evening. Put cotton wool soaked in witchhazel on your eyes, Clementine; they are looking a trifle fatigued."

"Yes, Mama."

"The maids will wake you at seven o'clock," the Countess continued. "That will give you an hour to dress and neither of you must be late. We will meet in the *Salon Blanc et Or* at ten minutes to eight. Is that understood?"

"Yes, Mama," Clementine said.

"And, Atalanta, see that your maid brushes your hair until it is completely smooth and tidy. I saw that there were some loose pieces around your forehead at breakfast."

"I will do my best, Aunt Louise," Atalanta answered, "but my hair curls naturally and there is very little I can do about it."

"Please do not argue, Atalanta!" her Aunt replied. "You have heard what I said."

Atalanta entered her bedroom and went at once to the window. She could see the whole layout of the garden.

There were flowering shrubs on either side of the lawn—lilacs in full bloom, azaleas, fuchsias, and a profusion of standard roses which she knew would shield her to a certain extent from anyone looking out of the windows.

"I will walk slowly at first," she thought, "until I reach the shrubbery. And when I am completely out of sight I can run."

She waited for fifteen minutes, and then knew she could wait no longer. The whole Embassy seemed to be silent and still. She crept to the top of the Grand Staircase.

Down below in the entrance Hall there were only two footmen on duty.

Boldly because she knew they would think it odd if she was at all surreptitious in the way she behaved, she walked down the stairs, across the hall, and appeared to be going to the Reception Room on the West side of the house, which contained sculptures and pictures.

When she reached it the room was, as she expected, empty and, passing though a French window, she stepped into the garden.

It was only a short distance before she could move behind the shrubs and the roses.

Again she did not hurry, just in case someone was watching from the bedrooms on the second floor. When she reached the shrubberies, she started to run.

The garden was quite large and Atalanta was breathless from the speed at which she hurried, for fear that she might be discovered before she reached the door in the high brick wall.

It was a stout, heavily hinged door and for a moment she feared it might be locked. But it opened at the touch of her hand. Outside she saw the scarlet and red of the sentry, and beyond him a closed fiacre.

The *cocher* was standing at the open door, obviously speaking to someone inside. At the sight of her he stood aside, Atalanta stepped in, and found Paul.

He put out his hands and took both of hers in his firm grasp.

The door closed behind her. The *cocher* clambered onto the box and the horses started off.

"You have come!" Paul said.

It was like a paean of joy.

"Oh, Paul!" Atalanta cried. "I did so want to see you again!"

Even as she spoke, she realised she should not have

sounded so happy, so eager, but it was too late, for the words were said and then he was kissing her hands.

Kissing first one and then the other, then turning them over, he kissed the palms, his lips lingering passionately against the soft warmth of her skin.

"I missed you," he said, and looked up to see her eyes wide and excited, her lips parted, the breath coming quickly between them.

"I ought . . . not to have . . . come," Atalanta murmured.

For some reason, which she did not understand, it was hard to speak.

"But you came," he answered.

"Yes, I know, but can you imagine what it will mean if they . . . discover where I have . . . gone."

"I had to see you! I cannot live, my darling, without seeing you!"

As before his deep voice made her feel as if something quivered within her. Half-afraid, she looked away from him. Instantly he freed her hands.

"I will behave, this I promise you," he said. "You must not be afraid of me, Atalanta. You are my guest and therefore I will behave as my Nurse would have wished, exactly like an English gentleman."

Atalanta laughed.

It was wonderful to be with him again—to see his handsome face, to look into his dark eyes, to feel excited and thrilled because he was close beside her.

She longed to put her cheek against his green-velvet coat and because she could not repress her gladness at seeing him she slipped her hand into his.

His fingers crushed hers until they were almost bloodless.

His eyes were looking at her as if he had never seen her before and she knew there was a burning fire smouldering in the depths of them.

"You are lovely!" he said hoarsely. "Even if I may not kiss you, I must tell you that. You are lovelier than I remember, so lovely that I am going to destroy the picture I have done of you and start all over again."

"You have finished my picture?"

"Not quite," he answered, "but I have worked at it almost every moment since I last saw you. And now I know it is not good enough. You are so much more beautiful, so much more exquisite, than any man could portray on canvas."

"Are you taking me to see it?" Atalanta asked.

"Do you want to come to my Studio?"

"You know I do," she answered.

"Oh, darling, I have dreamt of seeing you there. Have you thought about me?"

"Yes."

"What have you thought? Were you perhaps a little shocked because I kissed you when we said good-bye?"

"How did you know I felt like that?" Atalanta asked.

"I think I know everything you think and everything you feel," he answered. "You are a part of me. Have you not realised yet that we belong to each other?"

"It is . . . impossible . . . you know it is . . . impossible," Atalanta said.

"Is it?"

He asked the question, and with a tremendous effort Atalanta forced herself to look into his eyes.

"Quite . . . quite . . . impossible," she said.

She wondered why her voice did not sound firm and a little severe as she had intended.

Instead it was weak, soft, and breathless.

Chapter Five

PAUL was silent for a moment and then with a sudden change of mood he said, with a lilt in his voice, "We are nearing Montmartre. I want you to see my part of Paris."

He rose as he spoke and began to unclip the hood of the fiacre so that it fell back and they were in the sunshine.

"Can you manage, Monsieur?" the *cocher* shouted from the box.

"I can manage," Paul answered.

He pushed back the soft leather hood and now Atalanta felt the sun on her bare head and looked around in surprise.

While they were talking, they had left the Boulevards and the houses behind. Now they were climbing a steep hill on top of which she could see a number of windmills.

The crumbling, rocky sides of the hill were abrupt as precipices and dangerous to all except the small goats feeding on the acanthus clinging to the rocks.

As they climbed to the summit of the Butte, Atalanta saw green fields, arbours, rustic Elysiums, and little paths lined with cottages, barns, and overgrown gardens.

"It is the country!" she exclaimed with delight.

"It will not be the country for long," Paul replied. "Paris is encroaching every year. Already we have cafés, cabarets, and dance halls that are very gay and wild in the evening. Nevertheless one can still breathe fresh air here and work!"

At the top of the hill, there was a half-built Church in white marble.

"That is the Sacré-Coeur," Paul explained. "Soon it will be finished and there will be continual pilgrimages of people coming up the hill to pray."

"And where are the studios?" Atalanta asked.

"There—there—and—there," he answered, pointing to tall buildings, squat ones, and tumbled-down barns which had been converted into houses and small wooden huts.

"I see the artists have a colony here all of their own!" Atalanta smiled.

"We have found peace, a wonderful view, and a quality of light which is not possible in Paris itself," Paul answered, "what is more important than anything else: life here is cheap."

There was no doubt about the view. When the fiacre came to a standstill, Atalanta stepped out and stood looking at Paris lying below them.

She could see the grey houses, the straight lines of the new Boulevards, the silver of the Seine, the spires and towers of the Churches, almost as if it was a different world.

Then she felt Paul take her arm and lead her through a doorway and up a flight of dark wooden stairs.

"My Studio is at the top," he said.

There was a smell of onions, dust, paint, old age, and dirt. Atalanta had visited far too many cottages in her life not to recognize the last.

Then Paul pushed open the door at the top of the stairs and she gave a gasp of astonishment.

He led her into a huge room stretching the whole length of the building. On one side a high window seemed to occupy the whole wall. Atalanta had never seen a Studio before, but she felt this was exactly as she expected it would be.

At one end there was a small staircase which led to a room, where she guessed Paul slept.

There was a model's throne covered with a brilliant crimson piece of silk, a high stepladder, and everywhere half-finished canvases, stretchers, frames, books, and a coffee table on which there was a number of bottles.

Then Atalanta had eyes only for an easel in the very centre of the room, because it held a picture of herself.

The canvas was far larger than the one that Paul had painted in the wood, and as she walked toward it she saw that he had used his first picture of the Castle and the one he had done of her in the woods as sketches.

He had combined the two and now she sat among the daffodils in the park, the sun was on her hair, and the whole impression was one of suffused light, golden and dazzling.

Behind her, far away in the distance, and lost in a luminous mist was the Castle, having a fairylike quality about it as if it might float away into the sky.

It was undoubtedly herself, but yet an idealised portrait of her dreams, her aspirations, and her hopes.

"It is as I would like to be!" she said aloud, and then: "It is lovely, quite lovely! Surely people must recognise you for a great artist!"

Paul laughed.

"You are flattering me," he said. "Come and look at the pictures of my friends."

On one wall of the studio Atalanta saw there were some attractively executed murals. They had almost an eighteenth-century quality about them and yet they were modern.

They made the Studio seem larger and she felt she

100

was looking out into the lazy current of a river, the density of the water depicted in a marvellous infusion of light.

There were fluttering green trees, and she could feel the movement of the boats which were tethered to the bank.

"Did you do those?" she asked.

"I am hoping one day to be commissioned to paint murals on the walls of a private house," he said, "or perhaps a municipal building."

"I would love to have pictures like that in my house," Atalanta said.

"Then, who knows, perhaps you will give me my first commission?"

There was a note in Paul's voice which made her look at him sharply.

She had spoken without thinking, and now she remembered she was engaged to a wealthy important man and some of the happiness and excitement left her face.

As if intuitively he sensed what she was feeling, Paul drew her to the opposite wall, where Atalanta saw there were pictures hung from floor to ceiling.

Pictures of every sort and size. Some finished, some half-finished, some mere drawings or sketches on the backs of pieces of cardboard or even thick paper.

"Tell me what you like."

"Do they all belong to you?" Atalanta asked in delight.

"Some I have been given, some I have bought, some are exhibited here for sale," Paul answered.

It was difficult to know where to begin, Atalanta thought. Many of the pictures seemed to her very lovely.

She looked at one which represented a cornfield—golden with green trees all painted in that strange mysterious manner which seemed to light each leaf as if it lived and fluttered on the canvas.

"That is by Alfred Sisley," Paul explained. "He

painted it some years ago. He has never yet sold one of his pictures."

"It is lovely and this one is beautiful, too," Atalanta said, looking at a road in quite a simple village, all in shades of blue, which seemed to blend with the sky.

"Camille Pissarro," Paul told her, "but now he has turned his back on Impressionism. He has become aware of its dangers."

"And this one?" Atalanta asked.

It was a sketch of a man and woman dancing together. There were large gas lamps above them and a number of other people also dancing.

It had a movement, lightness, a gaiety that was irresistible.

"That is by the leader of us all," Paul explained, "Auguste Renoir. It was the sketch for his *Le Moulin de la Galette*, which caused a sensation four years ago."

Then Atalanta stood spellbound before a picture which seemed to her to bear a close relationship to the one Paul had painted of her. She looked up at him inquiringly.

"My master," he said, "Claude Monet—the master of Impressionism."

"It is beautiful, so beautiful there are no words with which I can describe it," Atalanta said.

"Someone said of him a little while ago that he 'raises sensation to the heights of revelation,'" Paul said. "Does that really mean something to you?"

"All these pictures make me feel more alive, happy ... perceptive," Atalanta replied.

"Thank you, darling," Paul said quietly. "That is exactly what I wanted you to say."

"I felt you would work in a place like this," Atalanta said, looking round her.

"If you only knew how I have longed to see you here! Walk about, let me watch you," he commanded. "Let me remember every expression on your face, every step you take, every movement of your hands."

Atalanta flushed a little at the note in his voice and

then he went on: "It would be impossible for me not to remember. Every woman that I see wears your face. Every sound I hear holds the music of your voice, every movement—even the wind in the leaves of a tree—reminds me of you. What have you done to me, Atalanta? I am bewitched!"

"I must not . . . listen to you," Atalanta said shyly. "You know I should not be here; it was just that I wanted . . . so much to see you . . . again."

"Do you really think that is wrong? Wrong to do what is instinctively right? You know we belong to each other, Atalanta, however hard you try to deny it. I am part of you—you are part of me. There is no escape for either of us."

She turned away from him to walk to the great window and stare out blindly onto the unkempt garden beneath them.

There were small wild roses growing over a broken wall. There was high grass blowing in the breeze and a white goat asleep under the shade of a silver birch tree.

She had a feeling that she would always remember the picture it made. A picture she was seeing from Paul's studio, from a room that was redolent with his personality.

She was conscious of him watching her, and because she still felt shy she said quickly: "I want to see everything. Can I go up the stairs and look at your bedroom?"

"Everything I own is yours," he answered with a gesture of his hands.

She crossed the Studio and walked up the somewhat rickety stairway. At the top, she stepped into the small room which was almost entirely occupied by a big divan.

It was very tidy, very neat. There was a small open window through which she could see the sky and there was one chest of drawers on which were laid, with almost methodical precision, a brush and comb and a case containing razors.

On the walls of the bedroom there were also murals, but they were of women, etherealised women touched with the magic of his imagination, who might, Atalanta thought, have been Goddesses, or perhaps portraits of women Paul had known.

She could not help a sharp stab of jealousy and she turned to come down the stairs again.

Paul stood silhouetted against the light from the window. His head was thrown back to look at her and she realised how handsome he was, how broad were his shoulders, how strong and authoritative he looked.

"How can I resist him?" she asked herself. "How can I ever refuse anything that he wants of me?"

She had an almost insane desire to fly downstairs and throw herself into his arms.

But then she saw her Mother's face, heard the twins exclaiming excitedly of what she could do for them, and remembered poor old Robin—Bernard's only mount—standing quietly in his stable.

It was as if they all besought her silently to help them, making an unbridgeable gulf yawn between herself and Paul.

Slowly she came down the wooden stairway.

"I must take you back," Paul said.

"Is it time?" Atalanta asked.

She knew they were talking conventionally because there was so much that was unsaid pulsating between them.

She wanted him to take her into his arms, she wanted to feel his lips on hers, she wanted, as she had never wanted anything else before, to feel that he held her safe and secure from the world.

But he was behaving like a gentleman and she knew that he would not touch her.

"We must . . . go," she said with a note of misery in her voice.

She felt in leaving the Studio that she was leaving something very important behind, something which

104

mattered more than anything she could ever explain
and yet was not for her.

Almost before she realised what was happening, they
had descended the dark, dirty stairs and he had helped
her into the waiting fiacre.

"It is very quiet. There do not seem to be many people
about," she remarked, because she felt she must say
something.

"All Paris is quiet between *cinq et six*," Paul replied.
"The French rise very early and then both the rich and
poor take a little breather before the excitement, the
business, and the pleasure of the night begin."

"That was why you knew that Aunt Louise would
send Clementine and me to lie down," Atalanta said.

"I was sure that at seven o'clock you would start
dressing for dinner," Paul replied. "I thought you might,
until then, have an hour or so to yourself."

"Can I come again tomorrow?"

"Do you want to?"

"You know I do."

"Then I shall be waiting."

Atalanta remembered how Paul had said these words
to her once before.

Would he always be waiting for her, she wondered.
Suppose the day came when he was no longer there?

She felt a little throb of fear and Paul said: "I would
so much like to show you Paris at night. I would like to
take you to *Le Chat Noir*, where all the artists go. It
is something unique that you will not see as you go
only from soiree to soiree, from social occasion to social
occasion!"

"Perhaps I could come one evening," Atalanta suggested.

"What are your plans?" Paul asked.

"Tonight the Ambassador is giving a dinner party for
us," Atalanta said, "and afterwards we are to go to a
Ball."

Then suddenly she clasped her hands together.

"I believe I shall be free tomorrow night!" she cried.

"The Duc is taking Aunt Louise and Clementine to the Opera. He asked William if he would bring me, but William said he was too busy. He has some important work to do. Aunt Louise said it was ridiculous for the Duc to escort three women, so I am to be left at home."

"Then nothing could be easier," Paul said. "As soon as they have gone, come to the door into the Champs Élysées. I will be waiting for you."

"Do you think it will be safe?" Atalanta asked nervously.

"I should tell your maid that you have a headache and wish to go to sleep early. If she finds your room empty, is she likely to tell your Aunt?"

"No, I do not think so," Atalanta said. "Marie is the girl who brought me your note. She had it hidden under her apron. She said the man who brought it impressed upon her that it must be given only to me."

"That was Jules," Paul said, "who looks after me. He cleans the studio and keeps everything tidy. I assure you you would not find everything so neat in any other Studio in Montmartre."

"I thought you could not have done it all yourself," Atalanta said. "I quite expected everything to be very untidy."

"And if it had been, would you have tidied it for me?" Paul asked.

"Of course I would," Atalanta spoke impulsively and now she turned to look at him.

"I believe you would not be too proud to wash, clean, and cook for the man you love," he said slowly.

"Do you suppose I have not done those things all my life?" Atalanta asked. "It would be no hardship."

"And yet my poor Studio is not good enough for you." Paul said.

"That is not true," Atalanta replied.

"Then shall I ask you to share it with me?" Paul enquired.

"No . . . no," she said quickly. "You must not say

106

such ... things. You know I am ... engaged to William. I have ... to marry him ... I have to."

She felt Paul stiffen beside her, and because she could not bear that he should be disappointed she said:

"You know if things were different that I would be happy to ... look after you ... to do everything for you, even to work for you ... if you were poor and could not afford to go on painting. But as it is. ..."

"But as it is," Paul continued, "it is easy to take the primrose path to riches, to importance, to becoming the Lady Bountiful to your family."

"You are being ... very ... unkind," Atalanta said in a voice that quivered.

She felt as if the sunshine had gone.

They had reached the bottom of the hill and Paul, calling the fiacre to a halt, stood up to pull the ancient hood back into place.

There was a smell of leather and of hay that was inescapable. But Atalanta was only aware of Paul sitting as far apart from her as was possible in the corner of the carriage.

There was a silence between them that was so poignant that it was unbearable. And, at last, with a sob, she put her hand on his arm.

"Forgive ... me," she said.

"There is nothing to forgive," Paul replied quickly. "I am being a brute to you and all I wanted was to bring you happiness, to make you enjoy the Paris that I know. It is only, Atalanta, that I love you so overwhelmingly I find it difficult to think of anything except our relationship to each other."

"Please let us forget all the other things when we are together," Atalanta pleaded. "I want to talk to you, I want to listen to you. I want to learn about the things you like, the things that interest you. It is all spoilt when we think only of the future ... and what I have ... to do."

"Forgive me, forgive me," Paul said and his voice was very contrite. "*Pardonnez-moi, my petite.*"

He took her hands in his and raised them once again to his lips.

"If you will come with me tomorrow night, I promise I will behave myself," he said. "I will talk to you only about Paris, although perhaps just now and again I will have to tell you that I love you. *Je vous adore, ma belle*, and I find it hard to think of anything else."

He kissed her hands and then, as he had done before, he turned them over and kissed the palms.

There was something about the hungry insistence of his lips which made Atalanta thrill as she had never thrilled before.

It was almost as if he were kissing her mouth and she was surrendering herself to him.

And then before she could say anything, the fiacre drew up outside the wall of the British Embassy and the sentry sprang to attention. Paul opened the door of the carriage.

"That man will not tell anyone that I have left the Embassy?" Atalanta questioned in a whisper.

"All Frenchmen enjoy a love affair," Paul answered. "I have explained to him that we are frustrated lovers, so there is nothing he will not do to help us. Unfortunately it is true!"

"I will come tomorrow night," Atalanta said quickly, "as soon as they have left for the Opera."

"I shall be here," Paul told her, and then she had moved away from him through the door in the wall and closed it behind her.

She walked slowly back through the shrubberies onto the flower-bordered paths.

"It will not matter if anyone sees me now," she thought. "They will merely think I am enjoying the fresh air. Nobody in the Embassy would think for a moment that, without a cloak, without a bonnet, I have actually been outside the garden."

There appeared to be no one about. Atalanta went upstairs to her room. It was a quarter to seven and quickly she took off her dress and lay down on her bed, so that when Marie came to dress her for dinner she would find her resting.

The dinner party was quite amusing, but Atalanta found it difficult to concentrate on the gentlemen on either side of her.

Only when one of them spoke to her of the Impressionists was she really interested.

"They are becoming more or less accepted," he told her. "The horrified disapproval which was shown by the critics and the public at Manet's *Déjeuner sur l'Herbe* has been forgotten, and now people merely shrug their shoulders and think the artists are mad. If they wish to starve for their art, who would bother to stop them?"

"You do not think they have something to say that is important?" Atalanta asked.

"Perhaps one would be more inclined to listen if they were not such unpleasant people," her dinner partner said loftily. "Drunk, drugged, quarrelsome, they are their own worst enemies. And they live like pigs. Who can be expected to take them seriously?"

Atalanta did not argue; she realised that this was typical of the aristocratic, and doubtless the bourgeois, attitude towards the Impressionists.

She managed to steer the conversation onto the New Art with quite a number of people she met, but not one of them had anything encouraging or appreciative to say.

She wondered at the end of the evening why no one could see the almost breathtaking beauty of Monet's pictures, the brilliance of Renoir's.

"Yet I have a feeling," she told herself, "that one day they and Paul will be famous. People will want to hang their pictures on their walls. Perhaps it is always the pioneers in everything who suffer, who are decried and perhaps even martyred for their beliefs."

Lady Fitzalan, who had acted as hostess for her brother, took the Ladies from the Dining Room, and

Atalanta learnt they were to go on to a party being given at one of the great houses of Paris.

She discovered that William was delighted that she had been invited.

"Tonight you will see the French aristocracy at its best," he said pompously as they drove along the Champs Élysées.

"I wonder if Prince Alexander will be there?" the Countess said to Clementine. "Did he mention it to you at luncheon?"

Atalanta looked at her cousin in surprise.

"You have met Prince Alexander!" she exclaimed. "Do tell me, Clementine, what was he like?"

"Very pleasant," Clementine said repressively.

"And you liked him?" Atalanta asked.

"We just met," Clementine answered. "It was a Reception given by Members of the French Senate to the Council of Vallon, so there was no chance for me to have any private conversation with the Prince. That will come later."

"If His Royal Highness did not tell you that he would see you tonight, I imagine he will not be there," the Countess said in a disappointed voice.

"The Duc will be present," Clementine said.

There was a sudden note of interest in her voice which made Atalanta glance at her sharply.

It seemed to her that Clementine was much more interested in the Duc than in the Prince. But then, she told herself, that was understandable.

After all, they had been together in England, they had traveled together, and he had been in constant attendance on Clementine ever since they arrived in Paris.

She wondered if Clementine would ever fall in love, and thought it unlikely. Clementine's head would always rule her heart; she had been so well trained by her mother.

The house in which the party took place was very impressive.

Inside the great Entrance Hall there appeared to be hundreds of guests all glittering with jewels and decorations, almost jostling one another to ascend the Grand Staircase.

There were turbaned Negroes in brilliant Tiepolo costumes to take the coats, the furs, and the wraps. The huge crystal chandeliers were blazing with candles, beside which ornate gas lamps seemed garish and out of place.

A throb of music came from the Ballroom and Atalanta could see long vistas of the room opening out of the main hallway, shining with mirrors and precious furniture, with lustres and pictures.

There were gorgeous Aubusson tapestries on the walls, flowers in enormous Sèvres vases, and the atmosphere was redolent with exotic perfumes, the scent of rich cigars, the fragrance of hothouse flowers.

William led Clementine up to their hostess, who seemed to be hung with diamonds, while virtually a crown of them glittered dazzlingly on her high-dressed hair. Atalanta was presented, she curtsied, and then William led her away into the Ballroom.

He danced well and they swept around the room in a dreamy waltz which made Atalanta feel quite romantic.

She was conscious of her new dress from London, which she knew was becoming, and that her shoulders were very white above the low décolletage outlined in chiffon.

"What did you talk about to the Duc de Gaumont at dinner?" William enquired.

Atalanta tried to remember for a moment which of her partners was the Duc.

"I think he was telling me about the Impressionists," she said, almost without thinking.

"Can you not find anything more intelligent to talk about?" William enquired. "Impressionists are not a subject for the dinner table. They are the laughingstock of Paris, outcasts, a collection of immoral revolutionaries

111

trying to force public attention upon themselves. Surely, Atalanta, you could find a better subject to interest the Duc?"

"I am sorry," Atalanta said meekly. "I cannot think how it happened."

"You are supposed to be intelligent," William said with the scolding voice of a schoolmaster. "Can you not realise that everything you say, as my future wife, will be gossiped about and discussed?"

"I had no idea I was so important," Atalanta said mischievously.

"You are not," he said sharply, "but I am! Kindly remember, Atalanta, that I am important because I own an ancient and respected title and I shall be much more important when I become Ambassador to Vallon. For Heaven's sake, be careful that you do not disgrace me."

Atalanta pressed her lips together. She wanted to argue with William.

She wanted to tell him how beautiful and how exciting she found the Impressionist pictures she had seen, and then she knew it would do no good, would merely infuriate him.

Perhaps some of the Impressionists were really as bad as they were made out to be. Paul was different.

She knew even without asking him that he neither drank or took drugs. She knew that he was upright and honest, true and decent, a man she could trust. But what was the point of trying to put that into words?

She was thankful when her dance with William came to an end. One of the Attachés from the Embassy asked her to partner him and she accepted gratefully.

When the dance was over she persuaded him to take her through the rooms so that she could admire the furniture and pictures.

She kept wishing Paul was with her. She felt he had an appreciation of beauty wherever he might find it. She knew he would not be bigoted as other people were against any one expression of art. There were so many modes, each in its own way beautiful.

"I will talk about it with him tomorrow," she told herself.

The Attaché at the Embassy introduced her to the other guests. She had one partner after another, they paid her compliments, and they made her laugh.

She found it was easy to accept the flattering things they said with a smile and even at times to be witty in a way she had never expected of herself.

She was laughing, happy, amused, and then as a dance ended she found William beside her.

"It is time to go home, Atalanta," he said. "My mother has already left with Clementine."

"Is it so late?" Atalanta asked.

"After two o'clock," William answered, "and I have to work in the morning."

"Then we must go at once," Atalanta said. "I am sorry I have kept you here so long."

"You have enjoyed yourself?"

"Very much," she answered, and knew it was the truth.

It had been amusing, it had been fun—after William had stopped scolding her.

One of the Embassy carriages was waiting for them. They drove down the Champs Élysées.

"You were quite a success tonight," William said. "Several people congratulated me on my choice of a bride."

"I am glad," Atalanta murmured.

"We must be married soon," William went on. "I suppose you would wish the ceremony to take place in England?"

"But of course!" Atalanta replied. "Papa would naturally want to marry us."

"That will be impossible," William said. "The Bishop of Chester is my godfather. He will be invited to conduct the marriage ceremony. I daresay your father could play a minor part in the Service."

Atalanta clenched her hands together. There was that note of contempt in William's voice that she had heard

113

so often from her Aunt, from her Uncle, and even from Clementine.

"Of course, the Reception must be at the Castle," William continued. "It could hardly take place in the Vicarage, could it?"

He laughed scornfully.

"Mama, with her usual generosity, will provide everything."

He waited and obediently, because she knew it was expected of her, Atalanta murmured: "That is very kind."

"And you can show your gratitude," William went on, "by watching Clementine a little more closely. She knows exactly how to behave. After all, she has done two seasons in London, and I could not help noticing to-night as we said good-bye that your curtsy to our hostess was not really low enough. You cannot be too polite, Atalanta, or too punctilious as regards details of that sort, especially in France."

"I will remember it in future," Atalanta said humbly.

"All the same you looked quite pretty."

William put out his arm as he spoke and drew her close to him.

"In fact, with a little trouble, you might be very pretty indeed!"

She felt his lips against her cheek and his fingers went to her chin as if to turn her face round to his.

Then with an inordinate sense of relief, Atalanta realised they were turning into the gateway of the British Embassy.

William realised it, too, and set her free. As they stepped out onto the red carpet, assisted by half-a-dozen flunkys, Atalanta dropped him a curtsy.

"Good night, William," she said and hurried away from him, up the Grand Staircase toward her own bedroom.

Alone with the door closed, she stood for a moment with her shoulders against it and drew a deep breath of relief.

He had been about to kiss her on the lips and she had known with an almost agonising sense of horror that she could not bear it.

She could not let him kiss her! She shrank from the very idea!

She knew now that she had held herself rigid and experienced something like disgust within herself from the very moment she had felt his arm come around her shoulders.

The implication of what she had felt was terrifying. She tried not to face it, tried not to express it even to herself, and yet it was there confronting her.

She took a step forward as if to throw herself down on the bed. Then remembering she was wearing the only smart evening dress she possessed, she checked herself.

As she did so there came a knock on the door.

"*Entrez*," Atalanta said automatically.

The maid, Marie, came in.

"I regret, M'selle," she said in French. "I did not hear you return. I have come to help you undress."

"But you should not have waited up so late; I can easily manage myself."

"Oh, no, M'selle, that would not be correct and I should get into trouble."

"It is so late," Atalanta said, looking at the clock on the mantelpiece, "and I am sure you have to get up early."

"Five o'clock, M'selle."

"Then you must go to bed at once," Atalanta said. "Just undo my dress and I will do everything else."

"But M'selle," Marie expostulated.

"I insist, Marie," Atalanta said. "It is very kind of you and I am very grateful, but you must have your sleep. We all need it. Now hurry get into bed and sleep even if it is only for two hours."

"M'selle is very kind. Perhaps one day I can do something for her."

Marie curtsied and went from the room, and

Atalanta took off her gown and hung it up in the wardrobe.

Then, as if something broke inside her, she ran across the room and flung herself face downwards on the bed, her face in the pillow.

"What shall I do? What shall I do?" she asked herself aloud and it seemed as if there was no answer.

Chapter Six

MARIE told Atalanta that she knew of a dressmaker who was *très chic et très bon marché*.

The Countess was pleased at the thought of spending less money and Atalanta and Marie set off the next morning to visit what Lady Evelyn would have described as "a little woman round the corner."

Marie had not exaggerated and Atalanta was delighted with the wizened, prematurely aged dressmaker who lived on the top floor of a house in the Rue des Pyramides.

Atalanta was shown sketches and patterns of exquisite materials and found that Madame Trevais was undoubtedly extremely cheap.

Being certain the Countess would approve, Atalanta ordered herself two evening gowns and a day dress to be made as quickly as possible.

Atalanta and Marie came carefully down the long narrow stairs from the top floor of the building.

As they stepped out onto the pavement of the Rue des Pyramides, Atalanta gave a sudden cry.

"Look, Marie!" she exclaimed. "Look!"

Opposite them on the other side of the road was a large notice saying *"Cinquième Grande Exhibition des Impressionnistes."* Marie appeared surprised at her excitement, but Atalanta said quickly: "Let us go into the Exhibition, Marie. I am exceedingly anxious to see the pictures."

They crossed the road and entered the long narrow gallery. The pictures were well hung at eye level and Atalanta started to go slowly round the gallery, entranced with everything she saw.

The play of Colour, the subtle infusion of light, the transcendent spontaneity, and the mystical blending of nature and realism were all there.

A number of pictures were signed "Degas," and were mostly of women in ballet skirts.

"Look, Marie, how graceful they are!" Atalanta cried. "How beautifully he suggests the movement of the arms and legs!"

Marie was not a particularly intelligent girl, and she stared at the pictures without enthusiasm. Atalanta moved on to examine several oil paintings by Camille Pissarro, who had also contributed fine etchings.

One painting of a landscape at Chaponel was of a sunlit hillside sheltering a village, while in the foreground a peasant woman tended her cows.

One can feel the breeze sting the grass, Atalanta thought, and sense the freshness in the shimmering light.

It was then, quite suddenly, that she saw a picture on the other side of the room which made her heart leap with excitement. There was something in the way the light touched the trees and seemed to ripple on the silver surface of river which told her, before she looked at the signature, who the painter was.

It was a painting by Paul. She had been certain of it at the first glance, and there was another bearing his name. This was of a young woman sitting on the bank of a stream, the vibrant strokes of the brush portraying the fiery gold of her hair.

It was difficult to see her face, but there was a grace about the slim figure which told Atalanta she was pretty, perhaps beautiful.

Atalanta felt an inexpressible jealousy, which became a sharp pain in her breast.

Then she heard Paul's voice saying—"I love you— *je t'aime*," and told herself she was being absurd! But he was so handsome, so attractive! Surely the woman in the picture must have loved him!

Atalanta was staring at the canvas, when she heard a voice say in English, with an American accent: "Is this the artist you were telling me about?"

"Yes, I believe Beaulieu has a future," was the reply.

The last speaker was obviously French, speaking somewhat hesitant English.

"You know, Durand-Ruel," the American said, "that I trust your taste implicitly. I will buy whichever one you think the best."

"Beaulieu is a pupil of Monet," the Frenchman said. "You see he has the same touch. He excludes black from his palette and has the same method of conveying light in its intensity and reflections. I already have two of his pictures in my own collection."

The two men moved away, and Atalanta clasped her hands together in excitement.

Paul had sold a picture and she wondered how much he would get for it. But she knew it was not only the money which was of importance, but the fact that he was recognised, that one person at least in a world of criticism and abuse thought he had talent.

She hurried Marie away from the Exhibition.

As they drove back to the Embassy, Atalanta felt she could hardly wait for the afternoon to pass so that she could see Paul and tell him what she had overheard.

How thrilled he would be and how proud she was of him!

119

The luncheon party at the Embassy was far smaller than usual. The only guest was the Duc d'Abencom, who had taken Clementine and the Countess to visit the Salon that morning.

Atalanta also wished to visit the Salon, but she could not help feeling pleased that quite by chance she had found the Exhibition of the Impressionists.

Because there were so few people around the table in the small Dining Room where the Ambassador ate when he was *en famille*, the conversation was general.

"Tell me, Duc," Lady Fitzalan said, "how far is Vallon from Paris? I know it is ignorant of me, but I have no idea."

"It is about eighty-five miles," the Duc replied. "It borders on Luxembourg and is a very beautiful country. I hope one day you will visit it."

"I hope that very soon you will ask me to do so," Lady Fitzalan said with a smile.

"It has wooded hills and lush verdant valleys, which is one of the reasons that France was so anxious to keep possession of it. We also make some very good wines."

"As I am well aware!" the Ambassador exclaimed. "In fact, your claret is one of my favourites."

"We are honoured." The Duc smiled. "Your Excellency must break your rule of never leaving the Embassy and come and stay with us as soon as we can make Vallon comfortable again."

"Did the German Occupation do much damage to your country?" Lady Fitzalan asked interestedly.

"We suffered so acutely," the Duc replied, "that it is best now not to speak of it! All our thoughts must be of the future, how we can reconstruct and make our people prosperous."

There was a note in his voice which told Atalanta that he cared deeply about Vallon. Then the conversation became general and, as luncheon was not a prolonged meal, Lady Fitzalan soon rose to take the ladies from the Dining Room.

Following the French fashion, the gentlemen went

with them into the garden. The Ambassador excused himself, saying he had a lot of work to do and the Aides-de-camp followed him back into the Embassy.

The Countess turned to Atalanta and asked: "Was your shopping this morning successful?"

"Yes, indeed, Aunt Louise. I have some patterns to show you."

"Show them to me now in the Sitting Room," the Countess commanded. "I have a letter to your Father to write, Clementine. I am sure you wish to send him your love."

"Yes, indeed, Mama; I only wish he could have come with us."

"Your Father hates travelling," the Countess replied, and led the way from the garden back into the Embassy.

Atalanta went with her Aunt into the Sitting Room on the first floor.

When the Countess heard the price of the gowns, she approved Atalanta's purchases and even told her she could have another day frock and one more evening gown. She was so pleasant that Atalanta was quite surprised until her Aunt said: "This morning the Duc was discussing Clementine's marriage with me. As we shall have so little time to plan a large trousseau, I think tomorrow, Atalanta, we must go to Worth and choose the bridesmaids' dresses. You will, of course, be one of Clementine's attendants."

"I should be very honoured," Atalanta said.

"And of course," her Aunt continued, "the gown will come in useful for your own trousseau. It will save me buying you at least one new dress."

"Yes, of course, Aunt Louise," Atalanta agreed.

The Countess obviously had no more to say. Picking up a white quill pen, she sat down at the *secrétaire* with a determined air.

Atalanta went from the room and closed the door behind her.

She was just going upstairs to her own bedroom when

she remembered, with a feeling of dismay, that she had
left her reticule downstairs.

She was not certain whether it was in the Dining
Room or in the garden, but it was important that she
should retrieve it immediately, because she had put
Paul's letter into it.

Yesterday she had carried his letter in her breast, but
this morning, as she thought she might have to try on
gowns at the dressmaker's, she had been afraid the
letter might be seen.

Therefore, for safety she had placed it beneath her
handkerchief in the little blue reticule which matched
the gown she was wearing.

She hurried downstairs and looked first in the Dining
Room, expecting to find the reticule on the floor beside
the chair on which she had been sitting. There was nothing there.

"I must have left it in the garden," she thought.

She went into the garden and found the reticule lying on one of the chairs which encircled a small white-
painted wrought-iron table on which the flunkeys sometimes set liqueurs and chocolates.

Atalanta picked up her reticule with relief. One of
the servants might have thought it belonged to the
Countess and taken it to her.

She wondered what her Aunt would have said had she
read Paul's letter.

The mere idea of such a catastrophe made her feel
quite faint. And then she remembered there were only a
few hours now before she would see him again. They
were going out together. She would spend the evening,
something she had never done before, alone with a man.

Almost without realising that she was doing so,
Atalanta walked across the lawn and found herself looking at the little path behind the lilac bushes which she
must traverse that evening to reach Paul, waiting for
her in the road.

It would not be dark, she thought, when she went to

him, but coming back it might be difficult to find her way.

Slowly, as if trying to memorise every step, she walked back to the Embassy along the narrow path, conscious of the fragrance of the lilacs and the roses and watching carefully for the turn at the end where she would enter the house through the French window which led into the big Reception Room.

She entered the room, wondering as she did so if the window would be open at night or if she must find a side door. Only when she was actually well into the room did she realise there were two other people present.

They were beside two of the exquisite statues which stood on marble plinths and at the sight of them Atalanta stood still in sheer astonishment.

It was Clementine and the Duc! They were clasped in each other's arms and the Duc was kissing Clementine passionately.

Only for a moment did Atalanta stare wide-eyed! Then, conscious that she was intruding, she turned and ran up the stairs to her bedroom.

"I was right!" she thought. "Clementine is attracted by the Duc, but what will happen now?"

She had not been in her room for more than a few minutes when the door opened and Clementine came in. She looked round, as if to be certain that Atalanta was alone, then shut the door carefully behind her.

She was always beautiful, but now she looked so lovely that Atalanta could only gape at her in astonishment. The coldness, the almost indifference which was characteristic of Clementine had vanished.

Instead there was a young girl vibrant and pulsating with flushed cheeks, shining eyes, and a mouth tender and warm from having been kissed.

"You saw us, Atalanta!" Clementine said a little breathlessly.

"I am sorry," Atalanta replied. "I had no idea that you would be there."

Clementine sat down on a chair and put her hands up to her face.

"Oh, Atalanta!" she cried. "What am I to do? I love him!"

"You love the Duc?" Atalanta asked almost stupidly, then continued, "But surely if he loves you, everything will be all right? The Duc can explain to the Prince that you have fallen in love with each other."

"That is what I want Lothair to do," Clementine said miserably. "But although he loves me as I love him, he will say nothing."

"Why not?" Atalanta asked.

"Because he says he must be loyal—loyal to his Prince, and to his country!"

Clementine gave a little sob.

"I did not know, Atalanta, that love was like this."

Clementine was silent for a moment and then she went on: "I have pleaded with Lothair; I have begged him to be honest with Prince Alexander and tell him that we need each other. But he says it is only Vallon that matters. Vallon! I hate the very sound of the word!"

"Oh, Clementine, you must not say that!" Atalanta said.

"You asked me once," Clementine continued in a low voice, "what would happen if the Prince and I hated each other. Well, I hate him, do you understand? I hate him because he comes between me and the man I love. I love Lothair, I love him and he has never in his life, so he tells me, loved anybody the way that he loves me."

"Then surely something can be done!" Atalanta exclaimed.

"What? What is there," Clementine answered, "except a life time of unhappiness for both of us? How can I bear to see him day after day, month after month? For he has to live in Vallon as there is so much for him to do there. Oh, Atalanta, I think I am the most miserable girl in the world!"

"I am sorry for you . . . very sorry," Atalanta said.

She could not help thinking that Clementine was expressing feelings exactly like her own. But at least she would not have the agony of seeing Paul every day; there would be eighty-five miles between them. And yet might that not be even worse?

Clementine was crying, and Atalanta put her arms round her.

"Do not cry, Clementine," she urged. "Perhaps the Duc will change his mind."

"There is no chance!" Clementine sobbed. "He has told me how much Vallon has suffered and it is almost entirely due to Sir Heatherington and the British Foreign Office that the French Government has been persuaded to change its mind and grant them Independence. It is also Sir Heatherington who has persuaded the Vallon Council of Ministers that an English bride would be a benefit to the country."

"There are other English women besides you," Atalanta observed.

"Can you imagine what Mama would say if I try to back out now?" Clementine said with a sudden panic. "She would murder me! She is so set on my being a Royal Princess!"

"The Duc himself is very important," Atalanta suggested.

"Perhaps Mama would accept him if it had not been a case of a Royal crown being dangled first in front of her eyes!" Clementine said. "And I was pleased, too, when it was first suggested. I did not know then what it was like to be in love."

"Poor Clementine," Atalanta said, but there was nothing she could say to comfort her cousin.

Clementine dared not stay long in her room because the Countess would be expecting her to go driving and she had to wash her face and obliterate all signs of tears.

But when later they all drove in the Bois with one of the Ambassador's Aides-de-camp, Clementine looked so unhappy that Atalanta felt her Mother must notice.

The Countess was, however, too busy bowing to acquaintances and talking of the parties they were to attend the following week.

Only Atalanta knew that Clementine's meek "Yes, Mama" and "No, Mama," were spoken from a breaking heart.

The afternoon seemed to drag interminably and Atalanta was glad when at last they could return to the Embassy and lie down before dinner.

Clementine was a little more cheerful because she knew she would see the Duc, as he was taking her and the Countess to the Opera. She dressed early and came into Atalanta's room, showing her cousin a friendliness which had never been there before.

"I feel unkind leaving you alone, Atalanta," Clementine said. "I cannot think why that tiresome William could not have come with us."

"I expect he is busy," Atalanta replied. "Please do not worry about me, Clementine. I have a very interesting book to read, and besides I have a slight headache and will be glad of an early night."

"It will be wonderful to be with Lothair," Clementine said softly, "but we must be careful, very careful. If Mama should suspect, I cannot think what will happen!"

She shivered and then unexpectedly bent down and kissed Atalanta's cheek.

"You helped me so much this afternoon," she said. "It was a relief to tell somebody what I was feeling, and I know I can trust you."

"Of course you can," Atalanta said, touched by the first expression of affection Clementine had ever shown her.

"Good night," Clementine said, and went from the room looking rapturous.

She was so lovely that Atalanta could not help thinking that it was a good thing that Paul could not see her at this moment, because then he might easily be convinced that she was the most beautiful girl in England.

She waited until the party had left for the Opera, then she rang the bell and told Marie she was going to bed.

"I do not wish to be disturbed."

"Very good, M'selle."

"And go to bed early yourself," Atalanta admonished her. "It is not often you can have an early night."

"No, M'selle, I will take your advice." Marie smiled.

She curtsyed and left the room. Quickly, Atalanta changed her dress. She had decided to wear a pretty blue gown which Paul had not seen and it had a blue-silk wrap to match.

It was not so smart that she would feel out of place in Montmartre, but at the same time she longed for him to see her looking her best.

There was always the risk that someone in the Embassy would notice her on the stairs, and wonder where she was going. But she had an excuse ready to say that, having a headache, she intended to walk for a little while in the garden.

Fortunately there was no one about, except the usual footmen in attendance in the Hall.

They paid no attention to her, and once again Atalanta slipped through the Reception Room, out through the French window, and down the sheltered path behind the lilacs.

She walked slowly, the skirts of her dress rustling behind her, until, as she reached the shrubbery, she started to hurry.

She did not run as swiftly as she had done the first time, but nevertheless she was a little breathless when she reached the door and opened it.

She felt a sudden fear in case Paul was not there. But the closed fiacre was outside and in a second she was inside it sitting close to him, her hands in his.

"Is everything all right?" he asked.

"Everything," she answered. "No one saw me leave! Oh, Paul, I have something so exciting to tell you."

"What is it?" he asked.

She told him how she had been to the Exhibition of the Impressionists and heard an American buy one of his pictures.

"It was Durand-Ruel with him," Paul explained. "He is an art dealer. He has been extremely kind to the Impressionists and has bought quite a number of our paintings. He almost bankrupted himself at one time because he could never find a client who would accept his own estimation of us! But now he is buying once again and I am honoured that he should recommend one of mine."

"Will you get a great deal of money for it?" Atalanta asked.

"Money is not the most important thing," Paul answered. "It is rather the fact that somebody, somewhere in the world, is interested in our work."

"I can understand that," Atalanta said softly. "After so many years of being abused and decried, it must be a great triumph to feel that you are accepted, if not yet appreciated."

"I wish there had been more of my friends in the Exhibition," Paul said.

"There were quite a number of pictures signed 'Degas,'" Atalanta said. "Do you know him?"

"Very well," Paul answered. "There is a chance you may see him this evening. He is usually at *Le Chat Noir*. Now tell me about yourself. Have you missed me?"

"You ... know I ... have," Atalanta said shyly.

He raised her hands and kissed her fingers one by one.

"I have thought of you every moment, every minute, I cannot tell you how different the Studio feels because you have been there. I can see you walking across it, standing by the window, coming down the stairs from my bedroom. Last night I went to sleep thinking of you, imagining you were there in my arms."

His voice deepened and Atalanta flushed a little at the passion which lay behind his words.

She knew his eyes were seeking hers, that strange fire in them which made her feel breathless and a little shy, but which she found irresistible.

"I love you, Atalanta," Paul said, "have you forgotten that I love you?"

"No . . . of course not."

"And you have thought about me?"

"Y-yes."

"All the time?"

She smiled at the insistence of his question.

"Nearly . . . all the time."

"Oh, my darling, if you only knew what it means to me to hear you say that!"

Paul kissed her hands again and then put them down gently in her lap.

"I have talked to myself very severely," he said. "I have told myself how well I must behave tonight, because I am privileged to take you out. Do you find it exciting, Atalanta, that we are alone together, that we are going to dine tête-à-tête, something which I am prepared to wager you have never done before?"

"Never!" Atalanta said. "I, too, was thinking how exciting it was as I dressed."

"Then, my sweet, we must make it a very memorable evening," Paul told her.

"Yes, let us be happy," Atalanta begged, "really happy, in case it should not happen again."

Paul did not answer, and because Atalanta was rather frightened at what she had said, she went on quickly: "I feel I must treasure every moment that I am with you, just as Clementine is doing."

She spoke without thinking.

"What is your cousin Clementine doing?" Paul asked indifferently, as if he was following a very different train of thought.

"It is a secret," Atalanta said, "although it will not matter if I tell you. Clementine is very much in love with the Duc de Abencom. He loves her, but she must marry Prince Alexander."

"Why?" Paul inquired. "If she loves the Duc?"

"Because of Vallon," Atalanta explained. "The Duc is loyal to his country and his ruler. I have never known Clementine to be unhappy before and, strangely enough, it has made her so nice, so human. I have never known her so kind."

"That is perhaps what love does for us all," Paul said.

"Do you think it makes you and me kinder?" Atalanta asked.

"I think it alters our whole lives," Paul said, "just as the Impressionists believe that light is what is important, and that it changes everything we see. So love like a blinding light changes us."

"I think I understand what you mean," Atalanta said reflectively.

"That is what I felt when I first saw you," Paul said. "You came through the park in the sunshine, and as I saw you it was a light striking deep into my very heart. That lovelight, my precious darling, changed my life."

"And you . . . think it will change . . . mine?" Atalanta asked almost beneath her breath.

"That is what I am waiting to hear," Paul answered.

The fiacre had pulled up outside *Le Chat Noir.* Atalanta had expected something strange, but certainly nothing as extraordinary as this tavern which had been started for a group of young poets and painters by a man called Rodolphe Sarles.

They were shown in through the narrow doorway by a scarlet-clothed Swiss, halbered in hand, and the customers were welcomed with exaggerated obsequiousness by a Master of Ceremonies.

"This way, My Lord! Will you take a seat, Monseigneur? What will you have to drink, Your Highness?" he cried in a loud voice to each new arrival.

Atalanta found herself in a large room which was decorated with Louis III furniture, with tapestries, pictures, church windows, stuffed stag's heads, armour, rusty swords, and worm-eaten wooden statues.

She looked round her, staring in astonishment as Sarles, the owner, with a pointed beard and wearing a tightly buttoned grey frock coat, welcomed Paul.

"*Bon Soir*, Monsieur Beaulieu. I am delighted to see you. Your table is waiting."

He led the way past a large table, already half-filled with diners, to a small one set in the corner by a huge fireplace which could burn a whole trunk of a tree at a time.

The tavern was lit with gas lanterns augmented with candles, which were alight on the tables. There were smells of roast goose, of tripe, onions, wine, and cigar smoke.

Rodolphe Sarles pulled out the table so that Atalanta could seat herself and she noticed that his fingers were loaded with rings.

"My friend Paul Beaulieu tells me, M'selle, this is only the second time you have visited Montmartre," he said. "Let me bid you welcome! Montmartre is the town of liberty! Montmartre the sacred hill! Montmartre the salt of the earth, the mind and navel of the world!"

He shouted the last words and a number of diners at the big table, who had obviously heard this speech many times before, laughed and cheered him.

Someone shouted for wine. Sarles hurried away and his place was taken by a waiter dressed in the uniform of an Academician. Paul offered the long hand-written menu to Atalanta. She shook her head.

"You choose for me," she said. "I am too excited to be hungry."

He obeyed her and after some consultation with the waiter, and then with the wine waiter, he at last turned towards her.

"Tell me who everyone is," she begged.

"There are not many celebrities here yet," Paul answered. "The man drawing faces with huge beaked noses on the table cloth is Jean Louis Forain. He is a cartoonist and has a certain amount of talent."

As he was speaking, a door opened and Sarles hurried forward to welcome noisily and exuberantly a man with a long oval face and heavy-lidded eyes.

He looked, Atalanta thought, like a Florentine painting, with a wide forehead and soft chestnut hair. He had full lips that were half-scornful and half-sullen and he

131

seemed to sweep Sarles aside disdainfully as he moved to a table in the far corner.

"That is Edgar Degas," Paul explained.

"I liked his pictures!" Atalanta exclaimed. "His ballerinas were lovely."

"He is obsessed with the ballet," Paul said, "although he is fond of drawing horses, also."

"They had a movement and a gaiety about them," Atalanta said, thinking of the paintings she had seen at the Exhibition.

Degas did not sit alone for long. Another man arrived to join him, and now Paul said, with his voice warming, "Now you will see someone I really admire. That is Auguste Renoir."

Atalanta looked to see a small man with a face of a fawn framed with a neat black beard. He was very thin and his eyes seemed sombre under a surface gleam. He waved to Paul then walked across the room towards them.

"Paul, I congratulate you," he said, "I've seen your pictures in the Exhibition."

"You liked them?" Paul asked.

"They are good! The best you have done! To borrow a phrase from Degas—you now are one of us."

Atalanta saw Paul flush with pleasure as he said: "May I introduce Monsieur Pierre Auguste Renoir—Mademoiselle Atalanta Lynton."

Renoir bowed to Atalanta, but before he could speak a girl approached from behind and put her hand on his arm to attract his attention.

"Monsieur Renoir," she said, "I am Marie-Clementine Valadon. May I pose for you?"

Renoir looked down at the girl. She was small and pretty with long, thick red hair. For a moment there seemed to be a gleam of interest in his hard dark eyes. Then he said abruptly.

"You are too young!"

"Too young!" Marie-Clementine ejaculated in surprise.

"Dear God! Don't you understand, girl? If I can't make

love to you, I can't paint you—you are only a child!"

"*Mais, Monsieur*, I am fifteen and I have posed for Pierre Puvis Chavannes!"

"That old goat!" Renoir said in disgust. "Very well, then, come and see me tomorrow. With that hair, I will paint you nude!"

"*Merci, Monsieur, Merci bien!*"

Marie-Clementine smiled ecstatically and vanished into the shadows. Renoir, without saying good-bye to Paul, started back to his table at the other side of the room.

Atalanta did not speak for some moments. She was thinking of Paul's picture.

Did he too find it impossible to paint a woman unless he made love to her? There was a sharp pain between her breasts at the thought.

The room was becoming crowded. Men poured in, some well dressed, some wearing ragged velvet coats with huge flowing ties spattered with paint or food.

They all seemed to have something important to say to each other; their voices rose noisily and their laughter rang out.

There were some women, but not many. But after a little while, Atalanta found it impossible to notice anyone but Paul. Although the food was good, they were neither of them hungry, and soon they were sitting almost sideways in their chairs, looking at each other.

"I never thought to see you in a place like this," Paul said, smiling.

"Can you imagine how shocked Aunt Louise would be?" Atalanta exclaimed.

"It is friendly," Paul said, "and when a man is both penniless and hungry he needs his friends. A large number of those here tonight will not be able to pay their bill, but their friends will stand them credit. They all believe that sooner or later they will sell a picture, or a miracle will happen."

"And if it does not?" Atalanta enquired.

"Then sometimes another body is fished out of the Seine," Paul answered, "and many of them go home.

There are young men here whose fathers are civil servants, shopkeepers, shipbuilders. When they are too hungry to go on working, then they go back to eat in Mama's kitchen and forget they were ever ambitious."

"You sound cynical," Atalanta protested.

"Not really," Paul answered. "There are others who are prepared to struggle on, to paint even when they are hungry, to hope when life seems utterly hopeless. That is what Monet has done and now at last, when it is almost too late, he is being recognized."

"Why is it almost too late?" Atalanta enquired.

"Because Camille, the wife he loved, died from the effects of starvation, from having children when she had not the strength to carry them, from continuing to love him even when there was not enough food in the house to keep body and soul alive."

There was something in the way that Paul spoke which told Atalanta that he was telling her this and making it a personal plea.

He was asking her, she knew, although he did not put it into words, to give him the same love that Monet's wife had given her husband. Camille had loved him and therefore she had been prepared to suffer for him, even if it meant her own death.

There was silence for a moment between them and then Atalanta said: "What is it that makes a man go on painting pictures that he cannot sell? Pictures which other people tell him are bad and worthless, and yet he still has faith in them?"

"I do not know," Paul answered. "Perhaps it is what we were talking about when we came here. The light of revelation. It has always been something to do with light which has affected man spiritually. It was a blinding light which converted Saint Paul. All through history, there is always a dazzling light when God or Angels appear."

"Yes, that is true," Atalanta murmured, thinking of what she had read.

"Monet said," Paul continued, " 'It is the vibrations

of light alone which give life and colour to every scene.'
I think, too, that like light the vibrations of love change
and alter our lives."

"Suppose they . . . cannot be . . . altered?" Atalanta
asked in a very small voice.

"We can change everything if we wish to do so,"
Paul said sternly. "Have you not realised that yet,
Atalanta, that our lives are our own? We make the pat-
tern of them, we change them as we wish; it is only
that most people are so feeble that they let themselves
drift. They do not control their own lives and that is
why they achieve nothing."

"And does one always have the . . . strength?" Atalanta
asked.

She was looking down at the table as she spoke, her
eyelashes dark against the pale fragility of her skin.

Paul looked at her for a long moment before he said:
"Are you so weak, Atalanta?"

She raised her eyes and looked up at him, a troubled
expression on her face.

"I am . . . afraid," she said.

"Of me?" he said.

She shook her head.

"No, not of you. But of jumping off a cliff, for that is
what it would be, as you well know."

He did not pretend not to understand her.

"And if I jump with you?" he asked. "Does that not
make it better?"

"I do not . . . know," she replied. "I am still afraid!
It is like walking a tight rope. I am afraid to go on. . . .
I am afraid to fall off."

"My darling, am I cruel to force you into making a
decision such as you have never had to make before in
your whole quiet simple little life?" he asked.

"It is . . . difficult," Atalanta murmured.

"I know it is," he answered, "more difficult for you
than for me. I have seen exactly what I want in a blazing light that has swept away the darkness, the doubts,
even the difficulties. It has put everything into its right

proportion. But you—you have not yet seen the light. When you do, you will realise there is no darkness for love."

Atalanta did not answer. She had never been so happy, she thought, as she was at this moment, sitting beside Paul, knowing they were close together.

Yet the doubts and difficulties seemed to overshadow them like the wings of a bird of ill omen.

It was hard in this strange atmosphere to remember her Mother. To think of her sitting at home in the Vicarage sewing or talking with her Father.

To think of the twins speculating about what she was doing, chattering excitedly about the presents she would bring them from Paris, of the gowns they would wear at her wedding.

And how in the smoked-filled noise and warmth of *Le Chat Noir* could she visualize the Castle, gaunt, majestic, aloof, waiting for her to become its chatelaine?

She felt herself shiver at the thought. The Castle was always cold and awe-inspiring. It had always made her feel insignificant and unimportant, yet one day it might be her home.

Then she remembered that if she lived there it would be because she was married to William. She recalled what she had felt last night when she had thought he was about to kiss her lips, and again she shivered.

Paul was watching her, and she knew that with his usual uncanny perception he was reading her thoughts.

"What makes you most afraid?" he asked softly. "The idea of the future with me—or without me?"

She looked up at him.

"Let me . . . think," she pleaded. "I must have . . . time. It is all so confusing. I feel as though my brain is going round and round in circles. Last night. . . ."

She stopped.

"What happened?" Paul prompted.

"I cannot talk about it," Atalanta said quickly. "Let us speak of something else. Tell me about these people;

tell me about yourself. What are you going to paint now that you have finished my picture?"

The words seemed to tumble over themselves, and then even her voice was lost as a mighty shout went up as a man came through the doorway.

He was a tall, blond giant wearing his tophat at a rakish angle, carrying his cane over his shoulder, and moving with a swagger.

"*Bon soir, mes amis!*" he cried in a gay voice.

"Who is it?" Atalanta asked.

"Guy de Maupassant, the writer," Paul replied.

"But I am reading a book of his!" Atalanta exclaimed. "One of the Aides-de-camp in the Embassy gave me *Boule de Suif;* it is fascinating!"

Even as she spoke, Guy de Maupassant saw Paul and came to their table.

"Where have you been, Paul?" he enquired. "I have been looking for you."

"I have been here most of the time," Paul replied, "working while you have been making yourself the most talked-about man in Paris."

"Is it not delightful?" Guy de Maupassant smiled.

"Everyone talks of you," Paul said, "*les salons, les vendeuses d'amour, les danseuses* in the Folies, every barge girl, every lock tender—they have all a copy of *Boule*! And eight editions sold out, I am told!"

"You flatter me," Guy de Maupassant exclaimed, "and I like it! Tell me some more."

Paul laughed.

"Atalanta, let me present this most conceited young man. Guy de Maupassant—Mademoiselle Atalanta Lynton."

Guy de Maupassant took Atalanta's hand and raised it to his lips.

"You are enchanting!" he said. "Why did I not meet you before this crazy Impressionist? Leave him and come and have supper with me!"

Atalanta dimpled at him; she could not help it.

"I am quite happy where I am, Monsieur, but thank you."

"You refuse me!" he exclaimed. "Do you not realise that after years of ignoring me, people are now fighting to talk to me? I am a success! *Le dernier cri!* What more could a man ask?"

"What more indeed!" Paul mocked.

"But you have repulsed me, Beautiful Lady, and my evening is ruined," Guy de Maupassant said to Atalanta in mock despair. "I must now drown my sorrows in Sarles's extremely bad wine."

He kissed Atalanta's hand again, his lips lingering provocatively against her skin, and then with a wink at Paul he moved away and sat at a table at the far end of the room.

"He is fascinating!" Atalanta said enthusiastically. "In fact he is just as I might have expected from his book. It is really brilliant! Have you read it?"

"No," Paul replied.

The monosyllable was sharp.

"He writes so vividly, so fluently," Atalanta went on. "I do not believe any author could describe a scene better or make their characters seem more real . . . the routed army—no longer troops but a loose mob; the Normandy countryside under the snow; the Rouennais bourgeois; the terror, the terrible irony, and the sharp, bitter comedy!"

Paul did not answer, and after a moment Atalanta looked at him.

"What is the matter?" she asked.

"We are leaving," Paul answered.

He drew some money from his pocket and put it down on the table.

"Must we go?" Atalanta asked.

"Yes," he replied.

He put his arm under hers and piloted her through the tables and towards the door. Sarles was busy at the other end of the room and the Swiss bowed them out, his halberd clinking as he moved.

The night air seemed cool and fragrant after the heat of the tavern. There seemed to be no empty fiacre waiting outside and Paul started to walk quickly along the road which led back to Paris.

He did not speak and after a moment Atalanta, who was struggling to keep up with him, asked: "What has happened? Why are you . . . cross with me?"

"I must take you back—we live in different worlds," Paul answered, and she was startled by the coldness in his voice.

She stopped beside a brick wall covered in honeysuckle. The moon was rising in the starlit sky and she could see his face quite clearly.

"You cannot be . . . angry because of what I said about . . . Guy de Maupassant," she said hesitatingly.

"You let him kiss your hand in that familiar manner!" Paul retorted. "You think him so brilliant! He is a success and I am not."

"Oh, Paul! Paul!" Atalanta cried. "How could you be so foolish? I admire his book, that is all. How can you think that any other man could mean . . ."

She stopped speaking as Paul put out his arms and drew her close to him.

"Finish that sentence," he said commandingly. "Tell me that no other man could mean anything to you but me. Say it because I have to know—I have to be sure."

She looked up at him and she felt herself tremble because his arms held her so close.

"There is only . . . you," she whispered, "you know . . . that."

Then Paul's arms tightened until she could not breathe and with a sound that was half a cry of triumph and half a groan, his lips were on hers.

He kissed her fiercely, passionately, and half-angrily. His lips bruised the softness of hers; they were hard, demanding, and possessive all at once.

Then, as if his control had broken, he was kissing her desperately—her eyes, her cheeks, her neck, and her shoulders.

For a moment she could feel nothing but the pain of his mouth, but then, as she felt her own lips respond, she felt an excitement and a thrill such as she had never known in her whole life before leap into life within her.

She wanted to restrain Paul, but it was impossible. She knew she had unleashed something uncontrolled, wild, and at the same time very wonderful.

"Oh, Paul! Paul!" she heard herself whisper.

Then his lips were on hers, again making it difficult to breathe and sending thrill after thrill through her until she felt almost as wild as he was.

Suddenly he raised his head.

"You love me," he said masterfully. "Tell me you love me! I want to hear you say it!"

"I love . . . you."

"And you are mine—mine! Make me believe it!"

Just for a moment Atalanta hesitated and then, because she could not help herself, she murmured—"I am . . . yours."

"Forever?"

"For . . . ever."

He was kissing her again, his lips seeming to set her on fire, until, as suddenly as he had taken her, she was free.

He took his arms away and she put out a hand to steady herself, feeling the softness of the honeysuckle beneath her fingers.

He walked away from her and stood looking out over the view of Paris which lay beneath them.

"Forgive me," Paul said and it sounded as if his voice was strangled in his throat.

Atalanta found it impossible to speak and after a moment, he said again: "Forgive me! I promised you I would behave like a gentleman, but you drove me too hard. I love you, Atalanta. I love you to the edge of madness and tonight when you spoke with such warmth of another man, and you so obviously admired him, it was more than I could stand. I have no excuse, only the fact that loving you is a torment worse than any hell the Devil could devise."

Still Atalanta could not speak. Then at that moment they heard the clop-clop of horses' hooves coming up the hill.

Paul turned his head to look, then he waved and a fiacre drew up alongside them. It was empty. Paul opened the door and Atalanta stepped in. He made no effort to assist her.

He gave the man directions and he sat in the corner as far away from her as possible. They drove for a while in silence and then Paul said:

"I am not going to say any more tonight, but I think we both know that the breaking point has been reached. I can no longer behave as if I were an Englishman with water in my veins instead of blood. I love you, Atalanta, and you have to make up your mind whether to send me away or marry me."

Atalanta would have spoken, but Paul put out his hand to cover hers. She felt herself quiver at the touch of him.

She was still tingling and aroused, as she had never been in her quiet sheltered life, by the fire of his kisses, by the fierceness by which he had held her in his arms.

"I want you to say nothing at the moment," he said. "I think the night has driven us both a little mad. Tomorrow you will be able to think and decide what should be done. I would not take you at a disadvantage. I would not force you, as I forced you just now, to say that you love me or that you belong to me. You trusted me and I betrayed that trust. Forgive me, my darling."

He raised her hand and kissed it very gently and, because he was so gentle, Atalanta felt tears well into her eyes.

Almost instinctively her fingers tightened on his.

"You are so sweet, so lovely, and such a child!" he said. "I am older than you, Atalanta, by nearly ten years, and because of that I must protect you. And if I were really doing my duty I should protect you against my-self. But I know we were meant for each other."

Atalanta gave a little sob.

"I think that . . . too," she said in a whisper, "but it is so . . . hard to know what is . . . right."

"I know, I know," Paul said soothingly. "And I am a brute to have ruined our evening together. I meant it to be so happy and gay. I wanted you to have a wonderful memory of my Paris—Paris of the painters, the Paris of those who have seen the light! Instead of which I have made you unhappy."

"No," Atalanta whispered. "I am happy . . . I promise you I am happy . . . it is just that I am weak, stupid, and afraid."

"You are none of these things," Paul told her. "You are perfect—half-woman, half-child. I adore you and everything about you. I respect you, I revere you, but sometimes your beauty makes me only remember that I want to kiss you from the top of your adorable shining head to the soles of your tiny feet."

Atalanta found it hard to breathe. The passion in Paul's voice made her long for him to touch her lips again.

Then he said in a very different tone.

"Forget everything that has happened tonight except that we have been together and I love you."

There seemed, Atalanta thought, nothing more to be said. Paul held her hand and they drove in silence for the rest of the journey.

Only as they drew up beside the door of the Embassy, did he say with, she felt, something like desperation in his voice.

"Promise me, Atalanta, promise me you will think of me."

"It will be difficult not to," Atalanta replied.

"And I shall be waiting for you tomorrow," Paul said, "waiting here and then we can try to come to a decision, Atalanta. Tonight I want you to sleep happily, believing only in my love."

The *cocher* had opened the door of the carriage, but Atalanta felt she ought not to leave Paul. She knew he was unhappy; the desperation in his voice was ringing in her ears.

However, there was nothing she could do but step out of the fiacre. She opened the door into the Embassy garden and heard it close decisively behind her.

There was an ominous note about it, as if she was shutting out something very important, something which mattered to her more than she could possibly put into words.

Then, as she stood listening, she heard the fiacre drive away. Paul had gone and she knew that he was as unhappy and perturbed as she was.

She wanted to call out to him, to stop him, and yet what she had to say she did not know. She only felt she was more miserable and more distraught than she had ever been in her whole life.

The tears were running down her cheeks as slowly, very slowly, she groped her way through the shrubbery back towards the Embassy.

Chapter Seven

ATALANTA woke very early in the morning and found her decision was clear in her mind. The night had taken away all her uncertainty and irresolution.

She knew as surely as if someone had written it on the wall that she could not go on living without Paul.

He was a part of her and she was a part of him, they belonged, and nothing else in the world really mattered.

She knew her Father and Mother would understand when she told them how much Paul meant to her.

Her Mother, after all, had done the same thing herself when she had refused to marry a rich and distinguished suitor and instead had chosen the impoverished man who held her heart.

Lady Evelyn had believed that love was more important than anything else, and Atalanta knew now that there was nothing in the world for her save Paul's love.

The twins might think she was selfish, but somehow, someday, she would make it up to them. Paul would become famous, she was sure of it, then she would be able to help Chryseis and Hebe socially.

In the meantime they would have to learn, as she had learnt, that money and rank were completely unimportant besides the ecstasy and joy of knowing that one had found true love.

When Atalanta got out of bed, she knelt down as she had always done and said her prayers.

"Help me, God," she said, "help me to be brave in facing what lies ahead. It is not going to be easy, but I know what I am doing is right."

It was the truth, she thought. Yet she was afraid not of her Father and Mother, only of Aunt Louise and of William.

She knew how scornful and contemptuous they would be. She knew the manner in which they would belittle her and find it almost impossible to believe that she should choose an unknown artist as her husband rather than the brilliant and successful William.

"I cannot tell them . . . alone," Atalanta thought in a sudden panic and knew that she must have Paul at her side to support her.

There was something so strong, so authoritative, about him that they would not be able to beat him down and humiliate him as, inevitably, they would her.

Atalanta had finished her breakfast in the Sitting Room before Clementine appeared.

The Countess had already eaten before either of the girls was up, and Atalanta knew they would be reproved later in the morning for being late.

Clementine looked unhappy and there were dark lines under her eyes which showed she had not slept the night before. When she saw that Atalanta was alone in the room, she said in a whisper: "Atalanta, I want your help. I must see Lothair today!"

"How can you do that?" Atalanta asked.

"Mama came into my room just now to ask why I was late for breakfast. She told me that we are all to go shopping this morning, but as this afternoon she is visiting an old friend, she suggested that you and I could go driving. We shall have to take a maid with us, but we could stop somewhere and I could meet Lothair."

"Of course!" Atalanta agreed. "The only difficulty is—where?"

She was trying to think, with her very limited knowledge of Paris, of a place where they would not be seen.

"I know!" Clementine exclaimed. "I will tell Lothair to meet us in the Bois. It would be quite reasonable for us to wish to go there."

"Yes," Atalanta said, "and I remember that Captain Bruntwood was saying that the Aquarium was well worth a visit."

"Good! I will tell Lothair to meet us there," Clementine decided.

She turned towards the door and Atalanta knew she was going to write a note which, by some secret means, would be conveyed to the Duc.

"One minute, Clementine!" Atalanta said. "If a maid is to accompany us, it would be best if we take Marie. I would not trust either Martha or Jeanne not to tell your mother what we have been doing."

"You are right!" Clementine said. "You ask Marie to come with us and order the carriage as early as possible after luncheon. Oh, Atalanta, how can I bear it? This is the last time I will see him alone."

"Why the last time?" Atalanta enquired.

Clementine turned from the door to stand holding on to one of the chairs which were set round the breakfast table.

"Do you not realise," she asked, "that tomorrow night my engagement will be announced to the Prince?"

"So soon!" Atalanta exclaimed. "I had no idea!"

"There is a special reception being given at the Vallon Embassy to celebrate the restoration of their Independence," Clementine explained. "Has not William told you about it?"

Atalanta shook her head.

"I expect he thought I knew."

"At the same time as I am officially betrothed to the Prince, it will be announced that William is to be the new Ambassador," Clementine said.

Then in a voice of utter misery she asked: "How can I face the future, Atalanta? How can I marry the Prince knowing that my whole heart belongs to Lothair?"

Tears welled into her eyes and she turned and ran from the room, being afraid, Atalanta knew, that someone would come in and see her unhappiness.

She was desperately sorry for her cousin and tried her best, during the morning which they spent with Monsieur Worth, to prevent the Countess from noticing how apathetic and indifferent Clementine was about the gowns that were being chosen for her.

More than once she was on the verge of breaking down, and Atalanta had to make a tremendous effort to draw the Countess's attention to some sketch or new material, so that Clementine could recover her self-control and avoid displaying her misery in front of her mother.

Fortunately, the Countess was particularly insensitive to other people's feelings, so that the monosyllables in which her daughter answered her evoked no surprise.

The gowns that were chosen for the bridesmaids were quite ravishing and it was easy for Atalanta to enthuse over them all the way back to the Embassy, and over the other dresses which they had fitted.

There were a number of guests at luncheon and Clementine's distraction passed unnoticed until they were free to set off for the afternoon in the carriage.

Then the colour came back to her face and the light to her eyes.

"Surely the horses can go a little faster?" she asked as they drove up the Champs Élysées.

"They are moving really very quickly." Atalanta smiled.

But she knew exactly what Clementine felt, because

she herself was counting the hours until she could see Paul.

She wanted to tell him what she had decided. She could feel herself thrill already at the thought of the expression in his eyes when she told him she would marry him and that nothing else mattered except his love.

But all the same it was impossible not to feel a little tremor of fear when she thought of telling William.

She had known, as she tried on the dresses the Countess had ordered her from Worth, that she would never wear them.

They can be altered for Clementine, she thought practically. It is only a question of making the hems a little longer and letting them out at the waist.

She did not regret knowing that perhaps never in her life would she have the opportunity of wearing such wonderful gowns.

It was only that she would have liked Paul to see her in them, to be aware of how elegant and attractive she could look when she was clothed in creations designed by a master hand.

"It is of no consequence," Atalanta told herself. "I must remind him to buy a small stove so that I can cook for him in the studio. And I will try to find some work by which I can augment the money that he makes by the sales of his pictures."

She knew that she could sew well and thought that perhaps there would be a demand for things that she could stitch or embroider.

She thought of how she would sit in the big window sewing, while Paul painted. It would be hard to concentrate because she would want to watch him, seeing the intent look in his eyes as he painted and the sudden leaping fire when he looked at her.

"I love him! I love him!" she whispered.

Deep in her thoughts, she had not realised that they had already entered the Bois until the horses drew up outside the Aquarium.

"You and Marie go in," Clementine said in an agitated voice. "I will wait here."

Atalanta obeyed her. With Marie walking beside her, she entered the large oval-shaped building and started gazing at the tanks of strange exotic fish from the Pacific, at great turtles, giant eels, and shy huge-clawed crabs.

The darkness of the Aquarium, with the light coming only from the tanks, made it a place of mystery, Atalanta thought, peculiarly suited to lovers.

She moved slowly and, finding they had completed the exhibits, she knew she dared not walk round again in case she and Marie encountered Clementine and the Duc.

She went outside into the sunshine. The carriage had waited in the shade of some trees, the horses shaking their heads and twitching their long tails against the flies.

"Let us walk a little way, Marie," Atalanta suggested.

They wandered across the grass to discover a grotto, a tumbling cascade, and a fountain throwing its water iridescently into the sun.

It seemed to Atalanta they must have been gone for a long time, but when they returned to the carriage there was still no sign of Clementine.

"I think Lady Clementine must have met some friends," she said to Marie, "but I should not mention to the Countess that we lost her. She might think it was our fault."

"I never talk, M'selle," Marie replied with a smile.

"I am sure we can trust you," Atalanta said. "That is why I asked for you to come with us this afernoon."

"You know I would do anything for you, M'selle," Marie answered. "You are the kindest young lady I have ever waited on."

"I am glad to hear that," Atalanta said. "Tell me about yourself."

Marie started a long story about how she had been brought up just outside Paris on a farm, how she had always wanted to be a maid in one of the grand houses, and how, having learned a little at the Château of the estate on which her father's farm stood, she had by sheer good chance been recommended to the Housekeeper at the British Embassy.

"Are you happy?" Atalanta asked.

"Very happy, M'selle," Marie replied. "They say unkind things about the English, but I find that they are kind to me and now I have no wish to work elsewhere."

It was sometime later that Atalanta saw Clementine come from the Aquarium. She was alone, and as soon as she reached the carriage it was obvious she had been crying.

Atalanta told the Coachman to take them home and they drove back almost in silence.

Clementine was fighting against a flood of tears, and when they reached the Embassy she ran upstairs to shut herself in her room.

Just as they were turning in through the Embassy gates, Atalanta had seen a man walking down the Faubourg St. Honoré with a huge basket on his arm in which there were dozens of twirling toy windmills.

Made of coloured paper they were a pretty sight, and Atalanta knew he must be on his way to the Champs Élysées where the vendors with balloons, windmills, and all sorts of attractions for children plied their trade.

"I am sure Lady Fitzalan's little girls would love those windmills," Atalanta said to Marie.

She drew some small change from her reticule and put it into the maid's hand.

"Run and buy two for me," she said. "I remember, when I was a child, how thrilled I used to be with a windmill."

Marie hurried to obey her and Atalanta waited in the hall for her to return with one windmill made in bright-red shiny paper, the other in blue.

"They make one feel young and gay, M'selle," the rather staid Butler remarked to Atalanta.

She laughed as she went upstairs holding them in her hand, seeing that even the slightest movement made them whirl.

The Schoolroom was on the way to her own room and she stopped outside to transfer the windmills from her right hand to her left, so she could open the door.

As she did so, she heard someone crying.

She thought for a moment it must be Clementine and that she had come to the wrong room. Then she heard a woman's voice say: "But what can I do? It is more than three months and soon I shall have to leave here."

It was Miss Dill, Lady Fitzalan's governess, who spoke and then to Atalanta's astonishment she heard a man's voice reply and recognized it as William's.

"How could you have been such a fool?"

"But you promised you would marry me," Miss Dill replied. "You swore that you loved me!"

"You know as well as I do, Mary, that at certain times a man says a lot of foolish things which he does not mean," William answered roughly.

"But I was sure you did mean it! And anyway later when you said you had to marry someone of importance, you said you would still go on living here. What shall I do now? Where shall I go? You must help me!"

"Now look here, Mary, let us get this straight," William said sharply. "I am not going to admit that the child is mine."

"But it is! You know it is!" Miss Dill cried.

"I will give you one hundred pounds when you leave here. That should enable you to find somewhere to live, a place where the child can be born. Afterwards you must fend for yourself."

"But how? Who will employ me? What shall I do?"

"Listen, Mary, I am sorry about this," William said, "but you know full well that I cannot be involved in anything even approaching a scandal. We have had some happy times together, but now they are finished. You should have had more sense. You should have taken more care."

"But how? How could I do that? You said it was unlikely that I should have a baby."

"How should I know about such things?" William asked angrily.

"But where can I go? Oh, God, I wish I were dead!"

There was another outburst of weeping, and then William said abruptly: "I will let you have the money tonight or tomorrow."

Atalanta suddenly realized she was eavesdropping.

She had been so astonished, so astounded by what she heard, that she had just stood paralysed outside the door, unable to move, unable to do anything except listen.

Now she thought William might be leaving the room and she ran down the passage, the windmills twirling at the swiftness of her movement, until she reached her own bedroom.

She shut the door and stood against it, her breath coming quickly. Only then did she realise the full implication of what she had heard.

How could William do anything so despicable, so utterly bestial?

She had seen Miss Dill and known that Lady Fitzalan would not have employed her if she had not been a decent English girl with a respectable background.

Atalanta pulled off her cloak and bonnet automatically. She walked to the mirror to tidy her hair and at the same time she saw not her own reflection, but Miss Dill's stricken face when she had spoken to her in the garden.

"William must marry her!" she told herself.

She waited a little longer in her room until she was quite cerain that William would have left the Schoolroom, and then she went along the passage.

She listened outside the door, but there was no sound. Then she entered.

Miss Dill was sitting at the table. Her arms were outstretched in front of her and her face was hidden in them.

As Atalanta shut the door, Miss Dill looked up, started violently, and jumped to her feet.

"It is all right," Atalanta said softly. "I will try to help you."

The older girl stared at her; the tears had run down her cheeks and her swollen eyes were suffused with them.

"What do you mean?" she tried to ask, but her voice broke in her throat.

"I overheard what you said to His Lordship, just now," Atalanta told her. "I did not mean to listen. I came to bring a present for the children. But I did hear that you were having a baby. Oh, I am sorry, so terribly sorry!"

"His Lordship would not want you to know about me," Miss Dill said pathetically.

"But I do know," Atalanta replied. "And I am going downstairs to tell him he must marry you."

"He will not do that," Miss Dill said with a note of despair in her voice. "I was stupid enough to believe him when he told me he would. It was only because I was so crazily in love with him that I was prepared to believe anything. But I knew afterwards that I was not grand enough for him."

She paused and then, with a pathetic little sob, she went on: "I would not have minded his not marrying me. I was content just to love him, if it were not for the baby."

"Can you not go home?" Atalanta asked.

"No! No!" Miss Dill cried in tones of horror. "My father is the Minister of the Wesleyan Chapel in Hampstead. He would kill me if he knew what I had done."

"And your Mother?" Atalanta asked.

"She has never really cared for me. It is my brothers she loves."

"Would they not help you?" Atalanta enquired.

"They are young," Miss Dill replied, "younger than I am."

The tears sprang into her eyes.

"It is all my fault and I am ashamed, deeply ashamed! But I loved him so much—I still love him."

"I will talk to His Lordship," Atalanta said, her voice firm and resolute, "and, Miss Dill, I promise you that if he will not help you, I will. You cannot manage with only one hundred pounds and a baby to look after. Somehow I will help you."

"You are good and kind," Miss Dill said, "and it is horrible for you to learn about something like this when you are engaged. I would never have told you if you had not found out. I do not wish to make trouble. You know that, Miss Lynton?"

"Of course I know it," Atalanta answered. "But do not worry about me, Miss Dill, it is you we have to think about now."

Impulsively she went forward and kissed Mary Dill's cheek.

"You are kind, so kind!" Mary Dill whispered and then the tears flowed again and she put her hands up to her eyes.

Atalanta glanced at the clock on the mantelpiece. It was a few minutes after four-thirty.

I will speak to William now, she thought, and felt that Mary Dill's misery had given her a courage she did not know she possessed.

She walked down the stairs. She knew where the office was which William shared with Sir Heatherington Houghton, and she hoped that he would be alone.

The office was down a long passage and there appeared to be no one about. Atalanta knocked at the door and William's voice said: "Come in."

He was sitting behind a big desk which was covered with papers and the other desk in the room was empty. He looked up as she entered and rose slowly to his feet.

"Atalanta!" he exclaimed in surprise. "I was just going to send for you."

"I want to speak to you, William," Atalanta said, advancing across the room until she stood at the side of the desk.

William did not answer, and she went on: "I overheard what you were saying just now to Miss Dill."

She saw the wariness of his expression as his eyes narrowed.

154

"Were you listening at the door like a servant?" he asked.

"I was listening at the door because I stopped at the Schoolroom to see the children," Atalanta answered. "I did not wish to listen, William, but now that I have heard that Miss Dill is having a baby, I must insist that you marry her."

"You insist!" William exclaimed incredulously.

"You need a wife," Atalanta replied, "but I assure you that I do not intend to marry you knowing your obligation to another woman. It is your baby, William, and it is only right that you should make it legitimate."

William stood staring at her for one moment and then he reached out and slapped her hard across the face with his hand.

Atalanta staggered and gave a shrill cry of astonishment and pain.

"You hypocritical little slut!" William stormed. "How dare you speak to me in such a manner! How dare you criticise my behaviour when I have every reason to be disgusted by yours."

Atalanta put her hand to her cheek.

"You . . . hit . . . me!" she said, and there was surprise rather than accusation in her voice.

"And I will hit you again," William retorted, "if I find you consorting with those dirty, drunken, immoral Impressionists."

His voice was thick with anger and he went on in a lower tone: "What do you think I felt this afternoon, when I accompanied an American Senator and an Art Dealer to view a collection of pictures in Montmartre?"

Atalanta gave a little exclamation, and he continued.

"I see that you know what I am speaking about! What did I find in a studio belonging to one of those filthy artists, but a picture of my future wife with my own Castle in the background! There was no chance of my not recognizing it, was there, Atalanta?"

William asked the question and then with his clenched fist he hammered on the desk.

"How could you deceive me in such a manner? How could you consort with men who are so low that they are the scorn of every decent-minded sensible Frenchman, men who are outcasts, drunk, drugged, and devoid of morals?"

He paused a moment and then went on.

"Their morals are beyond description, and yet you, Atalanta, dare to come to me and tell me to make a child whose paternity I do not acknowledge legitimate."

With a tremendous effort, Atalanta found her voice.

"There is ... nothing for me to ... say, William, except ... that I will not ... marry you."

William threw back his head and laughed. His face was still contorted with rage and his laughter had no humour in it.

"You will not marry me because you disapprove of my behaviour. That comes well from a woman who has consorted with an Impressionist! Is he your lover?"

He snapped the question at her and for a moment Atalanta did not realise the full implication of what he asked.

Then, as she understood, the colour flowed into her cheeks.

"No, of course not!" she answered furiously. "He is not like you ... he wants to marry me."

"And what will you live on?" William asked. "Do you not consider it beneath your dignity to beg in the streets? Or perhaps you will sell yourself to other impoverished artists so that you can eat."

He seemed to spit the words at her and in disgust Atalanta turned to leave him.

"I have nothing more to ... say, William," she said, her voice trembling, "except that you should ... marry Miss Dill. I have no intention of becoming ... your wife."

"Before you leave me," William said, and now he spoke in a quieter and, it seemed to her, more dangerous tone, "may I point out to you the implications of what you have just said? You have stated you will not marry me, but I brought you here for a purpose and that purpose is not fulfilled."

"You are to be Ambassador to Vallon, and you have to be married," Atalanta said scornfully. "There is a wife waiting for you upstairs."

"I have chosen you," William said and now his voice seemed almost suave, "and if you refuse me now, Atalanta, if you prefer this common artist, have you thought what results your decision will have upon your family?"

Atalanta turned her head to look him in the eyes.

"I shall tell my family the truth."

"I wonder if they will be interested in what you have to say when your lazy, incompetent father is turned out of his living," William sneered, "and I make quite certain that the Bishop does not offer him another one."

Atalanta was still for a moment, and then she said in a voice that was hardly above a whisper, "You . . . cannot do . . . that!"

"I shall certainly do it!" William replied. "You do not suppose that your father's neglect of the Parish has not been noted. If he were thrown out of Little Combe, I assure you that he would find it impossible to find another patron."

Atalanta did not speak and William went on.

"Bernard, of course, would have to leave Oxford. He is a strapping young man, so I dare say he can get a job as a farm labourer."

"You cannot . . . mean it!" Atalanta cried.

"I am not speaking idly," William replied. "If you do not marry me, Atalanta, then I assure you that you will find my threats are very speedily changed into action. Your family will starve. I wonder if then you will feel so high-souled about my behaviour?"

"You cannot do anything so despicable, so utterly . . . heartless," Atalanta said.

"It is entirely up to you," William answered. "Either you marry me as we arranged, Atalanta, or your family will suffer."

Atalanta was silent and he went on.

"As for you, if I catch you seeing this Impressionist swine again, I will whip you as I would whip a disobedient dog. You have been spoilt, Atalanta. Your family has always allowed you too much license for a young girl."

His lips tightened.

"Furthermore, now you will behave with the propriety I expect of my future wife. It will not be long before we marry, and until then I will see you are very much more strictly chaperoned than you have been up to now."

Atalanta could not answer him and his eyes narrowed until they seemed to be mere slits.

"As for Beaulieu, he shall not get off scot-free, I assure you! It is not difficult in Paris to find apaches who for a small amount of francs will beat up a man and leave him, if not dead, then crippled. And as for that Studio you have patronised, it shall be burnt to the ground."

"No! No!" Atalanta cried in anguish. "You cannot . . . do such things."

"I shall do so," William said firmly, "and I assure you, Atalanta, that it will give me a great deal of pleasure."

"You are a fiend! A beast! And I hate you!"

As her voice rang out, it seemed to Atalanta that William looked at her for the first time.

He saw her eyes wide and frightened, the trembling of her mouth, the red patch on her white skin where he had struck her, and her fair hair curling riotously round her forehead.

"So you hate me!" he said slowly, a sudden glint in his eyes. "Well, it will be amusing to make you change your mind!"

He moved towards her, and before she knew what was happening he had put one arm round her and with his other hand forced her face up to his.

She attempted to struggle, but it was too late; she was too small and completely ineffective against his strength.

Then his lips were on hers and she felt horror and disgust, as if something foul and dirty dragged her down into the gutter.

There was something bestial in his kiss, something which even in her innocence she knew was lewd and lustful.

It revolted her and yet she was imprisoned in his arms, and she knew that in some evil and unpleasant way her revulsion and her attempts to escape excited him.

Finally, when she felt almost as if she would faint beneath the cruel pressure of his lips, he set her free.

"Go to your room, Atalanta!" he said commandingly. "Think about your family and remember the whipping you will get from me if I find you seeing that artist!"

Just for one moment Atalanta tried to defy him, and then in sudden panic lest he should touch her again she turned and ran from the room. As she slammed the door behind her, she heard William laugh.

She ran down the passage and without thinking, without considering what she should do, she ran through the Reception Room out of the French window and down the garden path which led to the shrubbery.

She did not even wonder if she should be seen or if anyone was watching her; all she wanted to do was to reach Paul.

Only as she approached the end of the garden did she wonder if it was too early and he might not be there. Then as she pulled the door open she saw the fiacre.

She ran desperately the last few steps, her fair curls flying out behind her, her arms outstretched. The tears were running down her cheeks as she threw herself into the carriage and then she was in Paul's arms.

She felt him reach out to hold her and she threw herself against him.

"Paul! Paul! You m-must get o-out of P-Paris," she stammered. "He is going to h-hurt you . . . he is g-going to p-pay m-men to beat y-you up . . . Oh, Paul!"

"Darling, what has upset you, what has happened?" Paul asked.

His arms were round her and it seemed to Atalanta

that they were more comforting than anything she had ever known.

"H-he is g-going to ... b-burn down the ... S-Studio," she sobbed.

"It is all right, my darling," Paul said, holding her even closer. "Do not tremble like that! You are not to be afraid. I am here and I will take care of you."

"You do n-not ... understand," Atalanta said desperately.

She lifted her head from his shoulder and he saw the crimson mark on her cheek from William's hand.

"What have you done to your face?" Paul asked furiously.

"He h-hit ... me," Atalanta said. "He hit me because he found out about ... us. He went to the ... S-Studio and s-saw ... my picture."

She threw her arms round Paul again.

"But it does not matter! Nothing matters except you! You must go away at ... once. And Paul, I cannot ... marry you."

She burst into a tempest of tears which shook her from head to foot. For a moment, she could say no more.

Paul held her very closely. She felt his lips against her hair, her forehead, and finally against her burning cheek.

"It is all right, my sweet," he said. "It is all over now! Do not cry; I beg of you not to cry."

It was a little time before Atalanta could control her sobs. Then she took Paul's handkerchief of soft linen and attempted to wipe away her tears.

"We must not waste ... time," she said. "Already he may be ... paying men to ... look for you."

She realised as she spoke that the fiacre had come to a standstill. She looked out and saw the silver of the Seine through the open window.

"I wanted to talk to you this afternoon," Paul explained, "so I thought we would sit here. But it is not important. Tell me exactly what has happened from the very beginning."

He drew her close in his arms as he spoke. Atalanta put her head against his shoulder.

"I was going to tell you this . . . afternoon that I would . . . marry you," she whispered.

She felt his arms tighten around her.

"You have made up your mind?" he asked quietly.

"I knew that I could . . . not live without you, but Paul it is no use . . . I have to . . . marry . . . William."

"Tell me why?"

"I was counting the hours . . . until we could meet," Atalanta began. "After luncheon, I went driving with Clementine in the Bois so that she could say good-bye to the Duc. When we got back to the Embassy, I went to the Schoolroom to give two toy windmills to the children, and as I stood outside the door, I heard Miss Dill, the governess, and William talking inside."

She paused and drew in her breath.

"I . . . learnt that . . . Miss Dill was his . . . mistress."

There was pause. Then Paul said, "Many men have mistresses, my darling."

"I know . . . that," Atalanta said quickly. "I am not so foolish or so ignorant that I am not aware that . . . actresses and women like that are often the . . . mistresses of rich men! But Mary Dill is a lady. Her father is a Wesleyan Minister and she is having a baby! It is William's."

Atalanta felt almost shy at telling Paul such things, but after a moment she went on:

"He had promised to marry her. Then he told her he must marry someone important because of his career. And now he has learnt that she is having a baby he is giving her only one hundred pounds and says he will have nothing more to do with . . . her."

Atalanta drew in a deep breath before she continued.

"I went downstairs to tell William he must marry her, . . . but he had discovered that you had painted me. He had been taken to your Studio by an American and an

Art Dealer. He said terribly untrue and unkind things about you."

"I can imagine what they were," Paul said grimly.

Atalanta gave a little sob.

"I told William I would not marry him, but he said if I refused . . . that he will turn Papa out of his living! That Mama and the twins will . . . starve and Bernard will have to . . . come down from Oxford. Oh, Paul, how can I let that happen to them?"

She hid her face against the soft velvet of his coat and whispered in a desperate, frightened voice.

"William also said that if I . . . saw you again he would . . . whip me as if I were a disobedient dog . . . and that . . . you will . . . suffer, too! He is going to pay some apaches to beat you, to cripple you, and to burn down the Studio."

Her voice broke on the last words and once again she was sobbing miserably.

To her surprise, Paul took her by the shoulders and moved her to the corner of the carriage. Then he turned round in his seat to face her, holding both her hands in his.

"Listen to me, Atalanta," he said, "and look at me! There is something I want to say to you."

She obeyed him wonderingly, the tears swimming in her frightened eyes and glittering on the ends of her long dark eyelashes.

"I want you to tell me the truth," Paul said in his deep voice. "Do you trust me?"

"You know I do," Atalanta replied. "I trust you . . . and I love you!"

His fingers tightened on her hands, but he still looked at her steadily, his expression very serious.

"I adore you for saying that," he said, "but I am going to ask you to trust me completely and absolutely, Atalanta. If you will marry me, I promise you that your family will not starve. I may seem to you a poor and unimportant artist, but I have relatives who are in better circumstances. I swear that if Cottesford carries out his

162

threat and turns your Father out of his living, then another place will be found for him. Do you believe me?"

"I believe . . . you," Atalanta murmured.

"And I think you and I might contrive together, my darling, that Bernard will not have to leave Oxford," Paul said with a smile that was somehow irresistible.

"You mean . . . you mean that I can . . . marry you?" Atalanta asked.

"I mean that I have every intention of marrying you now that you have made up your mind," Paul replied. "Do you really think, my precious, my wonderful little Goddess, that I would let you go?"

Atalanta felt as if the inside of the fiacre was filled with sunshine—and yet she was still afraid.

"I have also . . . promised to help . . . Miss Dill," she said, hardly aware of what she was saying, because her eyes were held by Paul's

"I know the Mother Superior of the Convent at Neuilly," Paul said. "She will look after Miss Dill while she has her baby and afterwards perhaps the Nuns can arrange to care for the child while she goes out to work as a teacher."

"You have the answer for everything!" Atalanta cried. "But you . . . are you quite sure that you will be safe?"

"I promise you, my darling, that your despicable cousin will not hurt me," Paul answered.

"Be careful!" Atalanta pleaded.

"I will be very careful, my dearest Heart, for your sake. And now we have to make plans."

"Can we run away now?" Atalanta asked. "Then I will not have to go back!"

There was an eagerness in her voice and her eyes seemed to light up at the thought.

"Do you mean?" Paul asked, his voice very moved, "that you would come with me at this moment, that you would never return to the Embassy?"

"You know I would," Atalanta answered, "if . . . you will . . . take me."

"Oh, my darling, you are so wonderful!" Paul said.

"But we are not going to run away; we are going to confront them. We are going to be brave, Atalanta, as you have been brave already—and tell them the truth. We belong to each other, and we are not afraid of them or anything else in the world."

"But if we do that," Atalanta said with a sudden cry, "they will not let us marry . . . they will send me home."

"They will not be able to do so," Paul answered, "because we shall already have been married."

Atalanta's eyes were very wide.

"You are going to marry me now, tonight?" she asked.

"I am afraid that it means, my sweet, if we want to prevent a hue and cry, and perhaps the police looking for you, that you must go back to the Embassy—for a few hours."

"But how can I come to you?" Atalanta asked. "Supposing I have to go to a dinner party?"

"I have a feeling," Paul said slowly, "that Cottesford will not risk being seen in public with you tonight in case you cause a scene; but anyway, if it is suggested, refuse. Say you are ill, that you have a headache. He will expect you to be slightly hysterical!

"Go to your room. At half after nine o'clock I will be waiting outside, and by then our civil marriage will have taken place in front of the Mayor."

"But how? How?" Atalanta exclaimed.

"It can be done by proxy," Paul replied, "but I know you, my Beloved, would want to be married in Church."

Atalanta moved towards him instinctively.

"I want to be quite . . . sure that I am your . . . wife," she whispered.

He looked down at her little face upturned to his.

"I will make you very sure of it," he answered, "sure that you are mine and I am yours for all time."

Then he kissed her.

It seemed to Atalanta that it was a kiss different from any other he had ever given her. There was a reverence and a solemnity in it. But she still thrilled to the touch of his lips.

"I love you," he said and his voice was very deep and strong. "I love you, Atalanta, and the only thing I want is that you should be my wife."

He kissed her forehead and then her eyes.

"I must take you back, my precious," he said, "first of all because I do not wish anyone to discover that you have been seeing me again, and secondly because there is a great deal I must do before we are married this evening."

"Oh, Paul! Paul! Is it true?" Atalanta asked. "I thought when I ran to you that everything was . . . finished and I would have to marry William."

"You have said that you will trust me," Paul said. "I swear to you, before God, that I will never betray that trust."

"I know that you are everything that is true and noble!" Atalanta whispered. "How can people like William say such wicked things simply because you are an artist?"

"There is good and bad in every walk of life," Paul answered. "Many artists are all that is said of them; others are just men who have dedicated themselves to a special cause."

He smiled and then he added: "And now I am dedicating myself to you, my Beloved. I dedicate my heart, my soul, and my whole life to making you happy."

"But I am happy," Atalanta answered, "happier than I ever believed it possible to be! But, Paul, suppose anything should go . . . wrong."

"Nothing will," he said soothingly. "And once we are married, Atalanta, there will be no reason for you ever to be frightened again. I will be with you; I will fight all the dragons on your behalf and—my own!"

Atalanta gave a little sigh of contentment and then Paul gave the order for the fiacre to turn round and drive back to the Embassy.

Only as they drew up outside the door in the wall did Atalanta cling to Paul's hand and say: "You promise you will come for me! You will not let anything . . . prevent you?"

"Nothing shall prevent us being married this evening," Paul promised. "Nothing shall stop me from making you my wife."

"That is all I want," she whispered.

Then, as he kissed her hands, she stepped from the carriage and went back into the Embassy.

Chapter Eight

ATALANTA reached the Hall in the Embassy without meeting anyone. She realised that, as it must be about half past five, everyone would be resting, and she walked quickly up the stairs to the Schoolroom.

The children were playing on the floor with their dolls. Miss Dill looked up as Atalanta entered and there was a question in her eyes.

"Can I speak to you for a moment, Miss Dill?" she asked.

The governess rose and led the way into one of the bedrooms. She closed the door and stood looking at Atalanta, a pathetic figure with her swollen eyes and drooping mouth.

"I am afraid, Miss Dill," Atalanta said gently, "that I cannot persuade my cousin to marry you."

"I did not expect you to do so," Miss Dill replied.

"But I promised to help you," Atalanta went on, "and I have spoken to a friend who knows the Mother Superior of the Convent at Neuilly. He is convinced that they will take you in until your baby is born. After that the Nuns might contrive to look after the child while you can obtain a position in a school or perhaps do private teaching."

Miss Dill clasped her hands together.

"Oh, Miss Lynton, how kind you are!" she exclaimed. "At least I now have somewhere to go. I had begun to think there was nothing for me but the river."

"You must never speak like that," Atalanta admonished her. "You must never even think such things. Remember your child has a right to live."

"Yes, I know," Miss Dill said humbly, "but I was so afraid . . . so terribly afraid of being alone in France and with no one to whom I could turn for help."

Atalanta realised that Mary Dill was the type of woman who would always have to lean on somebody or something.

A Convent was the very best possible place for her, for she was sure that the religious atmosphere and the faith of the Nuns would bring her the comfort of which she was so vitally in need.

"Stay here as long as you can," she advised. "Then tell Lady Fitzalan you have to return home. Before that you will have heard from the Mother Superior, and perhaps on your day off you could go and visit the Convent."

"Thank you, thank you, Miss Lynton!" Miss Dill cried. "I did not believe there was such kindness in the world as you have shown to me."

There was nothing more Atalanta could say. She went back to the Schoolroom and spoke to the little girls, who proudly showed her their dolls and then she went to her own room.

Now at last she could think of herself and feel a indescribable joy seep through her at the thought that tonight she would be married to Paul.

She knew that he had attempted to alleviate her fears by saying that once they were married she had no need to be afraid, that he would protect her, that William's threats would be no longer effective.

Nevertheless, at the thought of William Atalanta shivered! There had been so much venom and vindictiveness in his voice that she knew he would strive to carry out his threats.

Paul would have to leave the Studio and find somewhere else for them to live. How ghastly, Atalanta thought, if they awoke to find it burning and were perhaps unable to escape.

Then she knew that when Paul's arms were round her she would not be afraid, despite the fact he was poor and unimportant while William was rich and powerful.

Yet she was not so foolish as not to realise how very dangerous a Nobleman of William's standing, with his diplomatic background, could be even in Paris.

"We must go somewhere else in France," Atalanta thought, and knew she would find it impossible not to be afraid if Paul left her alone, even for only a few hours.

Resolutely she put such thoughts away from her and tried to think only of what lay immediately ahead. She took off her dress and rang the bell for Marie.

"I would like a bath, Marie," she said when the maid appeared.

There was a bathroom on the second floor at the end of the passage.

The Countess and older guests staying in the Embassy bathed in their own rooms except those so important as to be given Princess Pauline's bedroom, next to which was her bath built into an alcove.

The Princess had had a mania for baths, as had all the Bonapartes. She liked to bathe in milk, but as it left a disagreeable smell on her skin, her Negro servant poured clear water on her from an aperture in the room above.

Marie drew Atalanta a bath. Having bathed, she went back to her bedroom and brushed her hair until it shone like silk and had an elasticity about it which made all the little curls spring into life.

Then Atalanta went to her wardrobe and stood looking at the gowns that hung there. Although she had the two new evening gowns which had come from London, she felt a curious reluctance to wear them.

They had been bought because she was to be William's wife and she felt somehow it would be cheating to wear them when she married Paul.

Finally she decided she would wear one of Clementine's gowns which had been sent to the Vicarage and which her mother had altered so skillfully.

There was one which Atalanta thought was particularly becoming. It was of heavy white silk draped with white chiffon, which fell behind her in a cascade of frills.

Chiffon-trimmed, the low *décolletage* on the gown accentuated her tiny waist. Atalanta knew she would look very young and bridelike in it, and that her appearance would bring a gleam of admiration to Paul's eyes.

She wished she had a wreath to wear in her hair, but although Clementine had dozens of them she did not dare ask her cousin to lend her one.

It might sound suspicious because it would soon be time to tell the Countess that she was feeling ill and wished to have her supper upstairs.

She tried to remember what they were supposed to be doing that evening and finally decided that they must, at any rate, be dining at the Embassy.

She had a sudden fear of someone in the dinner party seeing her leave the house to meet Paul, and told herself she must be extremely careful.

Atalanta was lying on top of her bed, planning exactly what she would do, when the door opened and the Countess came into the room. She was already dressed for dinner and was glittering with jewels.

Atalanta, who was wearing a muslin wrap over her nightgown, rose quickly to her feet.

The Countess shut the door behind her.

"I think you know what I am going to say to you, Atalanta," she said ominously.

Atalanta did not answer and the Countess continued.

170

"I am appalled at your behaviour! How you could lower yourself to sit for your portrait by some common artist I cannot imagine. I need not tell you that my son is deeply distressed by your behaviour."

The Countess paused, but Atalanta still said nothing. She only stood looking at her aunt, her hands clasping the muslin wrap around her body, her eyes wide in her pale face.

"When we return to England I shall tell your mother of your misdemeanour," the Countess went on, "and I shall point out to her that this is what comes of allowing you to run wild, walking about the countryside without a chaperone. She will doubtless be surprised at your perfidy, for I am convinced that you have deceived her as you have deceived me!"

She waited, obviously expecting Atalanta to answer her.

"I did not tell . . . Mama."

"Then I am sure your duplicity will come as a surprise to her as it has to me!" the Countess retorted. "I thought better of you, Atalanta, if only because you have the blood of the Combes in your veins."

"I am sorry, Aunt Louise, if it has upset you," Atalanta murmured.

"If I had my way," the Countess went on, "I would send you home immediately. Your wedding to William would be cancelled and you would be taught a sharp lesson you would never forget. But William is so magnanimous that he is prepared to forgive you. He has, however, said that this sort of thing must never happen again."

"No, Aunt Louise, I understand that," Atalanta said.

It did not matter what she said, she thought. After all, in a few hours she would no longer have to listen to her Aunt's strictures or be expected to be grateful for William's magnanimity.

Just for a moment she contemplated telling the Countess exactly how her son had behaved.

But then she knew that it would not only be unkind to

171

Miss Dill, but that she could not bear to sink to William's level and cheapen herself by uttering threats or taking her revenge.

She cast her eyes down in a manner which she knew would be expected of her and tried to look penitent.

"It is unfortunate," the Countess continued, "that William's first good impression of you should now be so damaged that I wonder whether he will ever be able to forget such reprehensible behaviour. However, he has said that he will forgive you and I must accept his decision. But, Atalanta, make no mistake, this will not be allowed to occur again!"

"I understand, Aunt Louise," Atalanta replied.

"In future you will not leave the Embassy at any time unless you are accompanied either by myself or by Clementine. I cannot even trust you with a maid."

The Countess paused to let her words sink in and then she continued.

"As you know, tonight William was taking us to the Comédie Française to watch a performance by Madame Sarah Bernhardt. It is something I am sure you must have been eagerly anticipating. But he feels, Atalanta, that you should be punished, so while we go to the Playhouse, you will stay at home. And I hope this will make you feel a little more contrite than you appear at the moment."

"I have already said, Aunt Louise, that I am very sorry," Atalanta said.

"I hope you will express your contrition even more effectively to William," the Countess snapped. "Your dinner will be sent to you here, Atalanta. In fact it is already waiting outside the door."

The Countess turned as she spoke and opened the door.

"Bring it in, Marie," she ordered.

Marie entered and put the tray down in front of the window.

"That will be all," the Countess said sharply.

Marie went from the room. Then looking severely at

Atalanta, in a manner which in the past would have made her feel fearful, the Countess said:

"You will eat alone and think of the enjoyable evening with us you will miss. As I do not trust you, Atalanta, I am, on William's instructions, locking you in your bedroom until tomorrow morning.

"When I awake I will send a maid to open the door. Until then you will be alone to think over your disgraceful behaviour and I hope be sincerely sorry for it."

The Countess turned with a flounce towards the door. Atalanta gave a little cry.

"No, Aunt Louise . . . please do not lock me in . . . I have an aversion to being . . . locked in a room—it gives me claustrophobia."

Atalanta's agitation seemed to please the Countess.

"If it upsets you so much, perhaps you will learn in future to behave in a manner which befits the wife of a future Ambassador," she said severely.

"Please . . . please! Aunt Louise, I beg of you not to . . . lock me in!"

The Countess left the room without heeding Atalanta's plea. She shut the door behind her and turned the key in the lock. Atalanta stood with her hands clenched while she heard her Aunt's footsteps going down the passage.

Then she rushed to the door, turning the handle violently, twisting it first one way and then the other.

It was a solidly made door and she knew that no force that she could exert could possibly open it. She crossed the room and sat down upon the bed in despair.

What was she to do?

If she could not reach Paul, he would be sure to think that she had changed her mind at the last moment.

She had been afraid that he might not come for her, she had never for a moment visualized that she could not get to him. She was locked in and now there would be no chance of their being married tonight!

Atalanta put her hands up to her forehead and tried to think.

"Paul! Paul!" She felt as though the cry in her heart

173

winged out towards him, begging his help, asking for him to save her. Paul would know what to do! Paul would find a way; she was certain of that!

She looked at the clock; it was half past seven. If William was taking his mother and sister to the theatre, they would dine at the Embassy and leave about eight o'clock. After they had gone, Atalanta felt she would find some way of escape.

In the meantime she was sensible enough to realize that there would be nothing to gain if she felt faint for want of food.

She ate the dinner that had been sent up to her, although she was so agitated she had no idea what the dishes were and if they were nice or nasty.

She ate with her thoughts on Paul, conscious of a rising fear within her that she would not be able to reach him.

Supposing he drove away, thinking that at the last moment she had been too fainthearted to contemplate a life of poverty with an unknown artist?

Worse fears arose to frighten her. If he left the Studio, which he would be wise to do because of William's intentions to burn it down, how could she find him? Suppose she never saw him again?

She felt herself tremble at the horror of the idea. But then she knew that, whatever else happened, Paul would never give her up so easily.

She had told him that she loved him, and even if he began to doubt the fact, he would still want to hear it from her own lips.

"I must get to him! I must!" Atalanta thought desperately.

She dressed herself in the gown she had chosen for her wedding, and looking in the mirror, realising that although her eyes were worried and she was very pale from a fear that was like a pain in her breast, she still looked lovely.

Her fair hair swept back from her forehead, and cas-

cading down her back in long curls, shone like sunshine
—the pale sunshine of the dawn.

"If only I can reach Paul," Atalanta thought, "it will be
the dawn of a new life for us both."

She watched the clock until it was eight forty-five.

Then with a prayer in her heart that her Aunt and her
cousins had left the Embassy, she pulled the bell which
hung on the wall beside her bed.

It was some time before she heard a knock at the door.

"Is that you, Marie?" she asked.

"*Oui, M'selle,*" Marie replied. "I am sorry I was so
long, but Her Ladyship told me you would not be re-
quiring me again this evening."

Atalanta went to the door so she could speak close
against it.

"Marie, is the key in the lock?"

"No, M'selle, Her Ladyship took it away with her."

Atalanta felt her heart sink.

"Do you think it is in her bedroom?"

"I don't think so, M'selle. I saw Her Ladyship put it
in the bag she was carrying on her arm, and then she
went straight downstairs. She didn't go to her bedroom
again."

"Marie, help me!" Atalanta cried. "I have to get out of
this room."

"But how can I help you, M'selle? I do not think there
is another key, and if there was the Housekeeper would
not give it me without Her Ladyship's permission. All
the staff know you are in disgrace."

"The staff know?" Atalanta questioned.

"Yes, M'selle. His Lordship was talking very loudly to
his mother in her bedroom and Jeanne overheard what
was said."

Atalanta was silent. She felt as though she was caught
in some terrible cage from which there was no escape.
She felt as if the walls were closing in on her.

Time was ticking by. Paul would be waiting and she
would not be able to reach him.

"I would help you if I could, M'selle," Marie said, "but what can I do?"

"If I cannot get out," Atalanta replied, "there is only one thing you can do, Marie, and that is to tell the gentleman whom I was meeting that I am locked in."

She wondered as she spoke if she was insane to confide in a servant, and yet had not Marie said she would do anything for her? Instinctively, Atalanta trusted her.

"I will tell him, M'selle," Marie said, "but where shall I find him?"

Atalanta looked at the clock.

"He said that he will be outside the door at the end of the shrubbery at nine-thirty," she answered. "Will you be there a little before that in case he is early, and tell him what has occurred? Ask him what I am to do. Tell him, Marie, that there is no other way of my reaching him unless he can break down the door."

"I am sure he would not be able to do that, M'selle," Marie said. "The footmen would be bound to see him entering the house and ask questions."

"Yes, yes, I know!" Atalanta said in despair. "Then just tell him that I am a prisoner. At least, he will understand that I cannot reach him this evening."

"I will tell him, M'selle," Marie answered.

"You know where the door is?" Atalanta questioned. "There is a sentry outside, but he will not betray you. I would not like you to get into trouble over this."

"I am not afraid, M'selle," Marie replied, "and you know that I would do anything for you. You have been kind to me, very kind ever since you have been here—quite different from most of the young ladies I have looked after."

"Then help me over this, Marie!" Atalanta pleaded. "Let no one stop you and do not let anyone see where you go."

"They won't see me, M'selle," Marie said. "I won't go through the garden. I will slip out and walk round by the road. That will be much the safest."

"That is clever of you!" Atalanta exclaimed. "And when

you see a fiacre draw up to the door, tell the gentleman inside what has happened. Then return to the house. I do not want you to be punished for helping me."

She felt as she spoke that if Marie was dismissed on her account, there would be yet another burden for Paul to shoulder.

She had given him so many already—her father, Bernard, Miss Dill—and to add Marie to the list was too much to contemplate.

"I'll do exactly as you say, M'selle," Marie promised. "And now I'll go downstairs so they won't suspect I have been talking to you."

"Yes, go at once," Atalanta said, "and thank you, Marie."

"Don't you thank me, M'selle," Marie replied. "I'm glad to be of service. And besides I hope you'll find all the happiness you deserve."

Atalanta heard the warmth in the maid's voice and smiled. There was no doubt that everyone in France loved a lover, and she knew that Marie was excited at the thought that she could help two people who were in love! And how true that was!

"I love Paul," Atalanta said aloud.

She loved him so much that the thought of not being able to reach him, because she was locked in her room, was an agony such as she had never experienced before in her whole life.

If William had wanted to punish her, he had succeeded; for the frustration and fear of not being able to reach the security and comfort of Paul's arms were more excruciating penances than anything he could possibly have imagined.

She sat down on a chair and watched the clock.

Nine o'clock came and it seemed as if the hands crawled at a snail's pace slowly, slowly, until it was nine-twenty.

By this time, Atalanta thought, Marie would be outside the Embassy walking down a side road to reach the Champs Élysées.

Nine-thirty came, and now Atalanta wished that she had asked Marie to come back to her and tell her what Paul had said. Instead she had told her just to give him the message and then leave immediately so she could not be involved.

It had of course been crazy to think that Paul could get into the Embassy and that he could break down the door and carry her away. The footmen and other staff members would obviously be able to restrain him.

There was nothing he could do, Atalanta thought, except perhaps tomorrow they could try again.

She began to plan how she could escape from her aunt and Clementine if they went shopping.

As they alighted from the carriage, she thought, and stepped onto the pavement, it would be easy to run down the street and disappear round the first corner, where Paul might be waiting for her in a fiacre.

She could imagine the astonishment and perhaps the hue and cry if she did such a thing!

Perhaps when she was able it would be easier just to go downstairs and walk out through the front door. By the time the footmen had obtained instructions from her Aunt or William, she could be streets away and could have found Paul wherever he was waiting for her.

But Atalanta was uncomfortably aware that any such action would undoubtedly involve the police.

And if the police caught up with them before they were married, then she knew she would be wrenched away from Paul and perhaps even, after all that, William would insist on marrying her.

"What am I to do? What am I to do?" Atalanta whispered to herself.

It was a quarter to ten. Paul would have gone, she thought.

He would have driven away, perhaps feeling everything was too much for him to combat, perhaps feeling as much in despair as she was herself about the possibility of their ever getting married.

At the thought, Atalanta put her hands up to her face

and then behind her she heard a sound which made her
start and turn round apprehensively, wondering what
could have occurred.

There was a sound of footsteps, and then, through the
open casement window, came first the legs and after-
ward the body of a man.

For one moment Atalanta was too astonished even to
wonder who it might be! Then, with a cry of sheer gladness, she ran across the room.

"Paul! Paul!" she exclaimed.

He was smiling as he stood upright in her bedroom.
And then his arms were round her and she was crying
with relief and sheer happiness because he was there.

"You certainly make things very difficult, my darling,"
he said and kissed her cheek.

"Oh, Paul! How did you do it? How did you get here?"
Atalanta cried.

He held her a little away from him and she knew this
was no time for explanations.

"Are you afraid of heights, my sweet?" he asked.

"No, indeed," Atalanta replied. "Once, because Bernard dared me, I climbed up the Church tower from the
outside. Mama was very angry, but I managed it quite
easily."

"Then, darling, are you brave enough to come with
me over the roofs of Paris, because it is the only way we
can get to the Church?"

"Climb out of the window?" Atalanta asked, wide-eyed.

"There is only a short stretch of a few feet which could
be dangerous," Paul said.

He took her to the window as he spoke, and she saw
that outside there was a narrow ledge with a small para-
pet no more than eighteen inches high.

Her room was at the end of the Embassy. Where it
joined the next house there was a buttress, and Atalanta
could see there was an iron ladder of three steps set into
the brickwork.

"All you have to do," Paul explained, "is to walk along
the ledge and reach the ladder. Climb it and on the

other side there is a flat roof and another ladder which leads onto the top of the house. There you will be quite safe, because there is a lead walk between the gables which will lead us over three houses to where I have found a way into a side road."

He paused a moment and then said: "But if it is too much to ask of you, my darling, I shall understand."

"Do you suppose I am afraid of anything," Atalanta asked, "except of not being able to . . . marry you this evening?"

"Then follow me," Paul said. "Hold onto me with one hand; steady yourself against the house with the other."

"Yes, I will do that," Atalanta said, her eyes on his.

He looked down at her gown and smiled.

"I think your train is going to be somewhat constricting. Can you pin it up?"

Atalanta went to the dressing table and found a large safety pin. She turned the train of her dress backwards, and pinned it onto her waist, being thankful that the petticoats that she wore beneath it would hide her ankles.

Then she turned towards Paul again and saw him watching her with a smile on his lips.

"You are very beautiful, my darling," he said, "and I love you more than I have time to tell you at this moment. Are you quite certain you have not changed your mind since this afternoon?"

In answer, Atalanta held up her face to his.

"Did you really think I should," she whispered.

He looked down at her red mouth inviting his, at her eyes warm with love, and just for one moment he laid his lips on hers.

Then as she felt herself thrill and instinctively move closer towards him, he said, "Come, my darling, we must not lose time."

He climbed out of the window ahead of her. Standing on a chair, Atalanta clambered out onto the narrow ledge which was only just wide enough for her feet.

"Do not look down," Paul admonished her and drew

her forward until she could put both hands on the buttress.

She climbed up the narrow ladder and onto the flat roof. There she saw the other ladder leading up the sloping roof of the next-door house. Atalanta knew it was used by the men who repaired the tiles and the chimney sweeps.

It was not difficult to climb and finally she found herself, as Paul had described, in a gully with two high-gabled roofs on either side of her.

He led the way, walking quickly, and she followed him, wondering if the people in the houses below them could hear their feet tapping away on the lead.

It seemed to Atalanta that they walked a long way between the gables until finally she saw an open skylight.

Paul climbed down first into an empty attic. Atalanta followed him, conscious of his hands guiding her, and as she reached the floor he held her for a moment close against him.

Then he pulled open the door of the attic and there was a narrow staircase going down in front of them.

There was no one about, but when they reached the first floor the stairs were carpeted and Atalanta was terrified lest someone should appear and accuse them of trespassing.

To her relief they reached the ground floor safely and Paul opened a door which led into the street. Outside there was a closed brougham. It was so different from the fiacre which Paul had used before that Atalanta stopped to look at him questioningly, feeling there might be some mistake.

"It is all right, my darling." He smiled. "I thought that for once, on such an auspicious occasion, we might be a little extravagant!"

Atalanta climbed into the carriage. As she seated herself she undid the safety pin which had held her train, then looked in dismay at her hands, which were dusty from the iron staircase and from touching the tiles over which she had climbed.

Paul drew a handkerchief from his pocket.

"I tried to think of everything a bride might need," he said, "but I never thought of white gloves! However, I have brought something which I hope will please you."

Atalanta looked and saw a lace veil and a wreath of real orange blossoms.

"How wonderful of you to think of a wreath!" she exclaimed. "I wished so much that I might wear one, especially as I was not certain if I would be allowed into a Church without something covering my head. But I did not dare try to borrow anything from Clementine."

"Let me put it on for you," Paul said.

He took first the veil and draped it over her hair. It was very beautiful and very old Brussels lace.

"Does it belong to your mother?" Atalanta asked.

"It did," he replied. "She is dead. She died of cold and starvation in the siege of Paris!"

"Oh, no!" Atalanta cried. "How terrible for you!"

"She would have loved you," Paul said, "and she would have wanted you to wear her veil today of all days."

"Perhaps she knows how happy we are," Atalanta said softly.

On top of the veil, Paul placed the wreath of orange blossoms and then Atalanta bent forward to look in the small mirror that was fitted to the side of the carriage.

"You have put it so cleverly," she said, "even better than I could have done it myself."

"I know how to make you look as beautiful as you are, my Sweetheart," Paul replied.

There was a throb in his voice that made her respond as if she was a violin in the hands of a Master.

"I remembered something else as well," he said.

As he spoke, he pulled a cardboard box from beneath the carriage seat. He opened it and drew out a small bouquet of white rosebuds and lilies of the valley.

"Oh, thank you! Thank you!" Atalanta exclaimed.

"Now I really feel like a bride. Oh, Paul, is it true we are to be married?"

"We are already married," he answered. "You are my wife in the eyes of the law and now, darling, we will ask the blessing of God upon our future together."

Atalanta drew a deep breath and he went on.

"It will be a very short service because it is a mixed marriage. I have never had time to tell you that I am Catholic. Do you mind, my darling, being married in Notre Dame?"

"Papa has often said," Atalanta replied, "that as long as we all seek God, it does not matter in what vehicle we travel in our attempts to reach him. If you are a Catholic, then if you would wish it, I would like, later, to become one, too."

Paul took her hand in his and raised it to his lips.

"How could I imagine that anyone would be quite so wonderful?" he asked.

He held her hand tightly in his and his eyes were on her face as they drove beside the Seine towards Notre Dame.

She looked at him, thought he looked different, and realised it was because for the first time since she had known him he had discarded his velvet jacket.

He was wearing the conventional evening dress of a French bridegroom. The spotless white shirt, high collar, and stiff cravat worn with the long-tailed black coat were immensely becoming.

He looked somehow older and more responsible, and at the same time so excitingly masculine that Atalanta wanted to throw herself into his arms.

But Paul did not attempt to kiss her, and she felt he was preparing himself for the solemnity of the service which lay ahead.

Paul had told her that he would dedicate himself to her and she prayed that she could dedicate herself to him with all her heart and soul.

Dusk was falling as they reached Notre Dame and there was a mystic exotic beauty about the grey-stone

Cathedral which was so insolubly linked with the history of France.

Paul helped Atalanta to alight and she looked up at the statues damaged and deformed, but which had still survived for so many centuries of time.

Then they entered through the great West door, and there was the sweet fragrance of incense, the flickering of candles in the darkness, the scarlet fire of the Sanctuary lamps.

For a moment, it was difficult to see until Paul, taking her arm, led her along a side aisle to a Chapel which was ablaze with candles and flowers.

A Priest was waiting for them and beside him were two acolytes in their red cassocks and lace-edged surplices.

At first Atalanta held her bouquet in both hands and then, as the service progressed, she set the flowers down as they knelt on the white-satin cushions of the *prie dieus* set for them in front of the altar.

Paul placed the ring upon her finger. It was a narrow ring and she was sure that it, too, had been his mother's. It fitted her, and the Priest, joining their hands together, declared they were man and wife.

The whole service had a dreamlike quality and Atalanta felt that she and Paul were encompassed by a host of angels.

The world slipped away from them and she knew the love they had for each other was touched by the Divine.

"Keep us safe, God," she prayed, "and let our love for each other always remain as pure and as perfect as it is today."

When the service was over, Paul, holding her hand, drew her to a table at the side of the Chapel on which there was a book.

Atalanta signed her name and stood back for Paul to sign his, and then they were moving again through the incense-fragrant darkness of the aisle and out through the great door to where the brougham was waiting for them.

"I am married! I am married!" Atalanta whispered to herself.

She put her bouquet down on the seat opposite them and turned to Paul, knowing without being told that he had been as moved as she was by the beauty and the solemnity of the service.

"Oh, Paul!" She could hardly breathe the words and he took her hand in his and held it against his lips.

He put his arm round her and drew her close, but still they did not speak. There seemed to be nothing to say in words that their hearts were not saying for them.

After a moment, Atalanta laid her head on Paul's shoulder with a sigh of relief that was more eloquent than if she had told him how wonderful it was to be his wife.

The carriage drove quickly away through the narrow streets and the brilliantly lit Boulevards. Atalanta knew they were going to Montmartre.

She could feel Paul kissing her hair and then his lips were against her forehead.

He did not raise her face up to his and she knew that for a moment the service in Notre Dame made them almost disembodied. Two people no longer on earth, but caught up into a special Heaven, their love a part of God.

Then at last the carriage drew up at Paul's Studio.

"Is it safe?" Atalanta asked, bending forward.

Even as she spoke, she saw several men standing in the shadows and shrank back against Paul.

"It is all right, my darling," he said. "Those are friends of mine; they are keeping a watch over us for tonight."

He stepped out of the carriage and helped Atalanta to alight.

His friends did not come forward to speak to them and they entered the house and climbed up the long narrow stairs to the Studio.

Paul opened the door and Atalanta went in ahead of him.

There was an almost overpowering fragrance of lilies and roses, and as she stared around her in surprise she saw that all the pictures had gone. There was only one left, the picture of herself.

It was set on a table opposite the door and at the foot of it were dozens of small candles. They illuminated the Studio and highlighted the beauty and the exquisite painting of the picture.

She found herself staring into her own eyes, seeing the sunshine around her, and the candlelight made the whole picture sparkle and shimmer as if alive.

Then Atalanta saw that the divan which had been in Paul's bedroom had been moved downstairs and had been put against the further wall which faced the window.

There were great vases of lilies on either side of it, and the piece of crimson silk which she had seen on the model's throne now covered the bed, and strewn over it were petals of pink and white roses and carnations.

Atalanta realised the whole Studio was fillled with great bunches of roses and carnations, just as if someone had bought up the whole stock from the little stalls of the flower women who offered their wares on every street corner and on the steps of the Madeleine.

Through the huge uncurtained window the moon was visible, rising up the sky and throwing a silver light into the Studio, so that the whole place was mysterious and enchanted.

But Atalanta had only a moment in which to take everything in as Paul shut the door and locked it.

Now he put his arms round her and drew her across the room to face her picture.

"You see what I have placed here, my sweet?" he asked.

"The picture of me," Atalanta replied.

"Your picture," he said, "and I have arranged it so that

it is a shrine—a shrine to you, my precious wife, and to our love."

She looked up at him wide-eyed, and he went on.

"I wanted you to understand, Heart of my Heart, that as a man grows up he gets to know many women and loves them because, like flowers, they bring beauty and fragrance into his life."

He looked down at Atalanta and said, with a little twist on his lips, "I saw your face, my dearest one, when Renoir said that he could only paint a woman when he had made love to her. And that is why tonight I want you to understand fully, and once and for all, that although there have been many women in my life, none of them has meant what you mean to me."

He drew in his breath.

"Always in my heart I have known they were not what I was seeking. They were not the perfect love which one day, I believed with unquestionable faith, I would find."

His arms tightened round Atalanta and his voice deepened as he went on.

"In you I have found the woman I have always, at first unconsciously and later consciously, been seeking. That is why, my wonderful adorable one, I have put you in a shrine—a shrine where you will remain forever —my love, my guide, my inspiration and my wife."

His words and the tone in which he spoke them brought tears to Atalanta's eyes.

Now, very gently, he took the wreath of orange blossoms from her hair and drew off her veil almost as if it was a symbolic gesture.

For a moment, he looked down at her face before he drew her closer, and even closer, into his arms.

"My wife," he repeated, and his lips were on hers.

It seemed to Atalanta as if an ecstasy as brilliant and penetrating as a flash of lightening carried them both away into the star-strewn sky.

The world was forgotten, they were no longer human,

but gods, joined together in a rapture that was indescribable.

"*Je t'adore*. I love you, *Mon Dieu*, how I love you!" Paul cried.

Then he was kissing her eyes, her cheeks, her lips, and the softness of her neck, making her quiver with a strange sensation she had never known before.

At first his kisses were gentle, until it seemed to Atalanta as if a blazing fire in Paul ignited a fire within herself.

Now he was kissing her wildly, more passionately, demandingly, possessively, every moment.

He drew the pins from her hair and pulled it over her shoulders and across her face, kissing her through the silken veil. She felt him unfasten her gown at the back and his lips were seeking her small rose-tipped breasts.

She knew that an irresistible force swept from her everything but the need to feel and thrill to the wonder of his touch.

And as she surrendered herself completely to his desire, he lifted her in his arms and carried her toward the petal-strewn divan.

It was later, much later, that Atalanta realised that the candles had guttered away and only two or three remained alight like fireflies in the darkness.

The moonbeams, silver and mystic, flooded the whole studio and she could see the stars glittering like diamonds in the sky.

She made a little movement and instantly Paul's arms were round her, drawing her close.

"Are you happy, my darling?" he asked.

"I did not know such . . . happiness . . . existed," Atalanta replied.

She pressed her lips against his bare shoulder and then she said in a whisper: "There is . . . something I want to . . . ask you."

"What is it, my sweet?"

His voice was low and deep with emotion and she

felt nothing could be more wonderful than to be lying close against the hard strength of his body, knowing they were one.

"You have . . . not been . . . disappointed in me?" she asked a little breathlessly.

"Disappointed?" he asked, "My precious, have I been such a bad lover that I have not convinced you that nothing in my whole life has ever been so absolutely and completely perfect?"

"I just wanted to . . . be sure that loving each other was as . . . marvellous for . . . you as for . . . me," Atalanta told him. "Oh, Paul, I feel that it was for this that I was born . . . I am yours . . . all of me."

"We have found each other," Paul said. "That is what matters."

"And suppose we had not?" Atalanta asked.

"Then we could never have been complete my beloved little Goddess, only unhappy, frustrated, and restless ghostlike creatures, looking for each other, perhaps not only in this life, but in many lives to come."

"Do not say it," Atalanta begged. "It . . . frightens . . . me."

"You are never to be frightened again, *ma petite*. Do you not realise that I am here to look after you, to love you, to worship you as long as we live?"

"I love you . . . forever," Atalanta whispered.

Then her mouth was soft beneath the insistence of his lips. She could feel his heart beating against hers.

His hands were gentle yet compelling and it was impossible to think any more; she could only feel . . . and feel . . . and feel. . . .

Later still, Atalanta opened her eyes and saw that the moon had gone.

The stars were fading, yet it was still faintly light in the studio. It was, she knew, the light which came just before the dawn.

She realised that Paul was also looking at the sky.

"Listen to me, my darling," he said. "I have something to say to you."

His voice was very serious and Atalanta said quickly, "Is there something wrong?"

"Nothing is wrong," he replied, "but I hate, my adorable wife, to disappoint you and that is what I am afraid I have to do."

"What do you mean?" Atalanta asked.

"We both know that we would want to spend the first day of our marriage together alone, to talk about ourselves. A day when I could tell you over and over again, in case you were not certain of it, that I adore you. But my precious, there is something I have to do —something which will be of tremendous importance to us both in the future."

"Do you . . . have to go . . . away?" Atalanta asked.

"I am afraid so," he said, "but only for today; we shall be together again this evening."

Just for a moment Atalanta felt that the disappointment was too much to be borne. Then she remembered that she was now Paul's wife and she must help him.

She was sure the important thing he had to do concerned his painting. Perhaps at last there was the chance of the murals he had longed to execute being commissioned. Perhaps someone important was going to buy one of his pictures.

With an effort, she made herself speak quietly and gently as she asked, "Will you tell me about it?"

"Not now," he said, "because like everything else I do in my life, I want to bring my triumphs to you and lay them at your feet. Will you trust me until I know this is a *fait accompli*? Then I will tell you everything, my darling, and hope that you will be proud of me."

"I will be . . . you know I will be," Atalanta said. "But what do you want me to do?"

"I cannot leave you here," Paul replied. "You do realise that? I could not go away, if I was afraid that something might happen to you."

"No, I could not stay here without you," Atalanta agreed, thinking that apaches sent by William might come and burn down the studio.

"Then forgive me if what I am asking is too much," Paul said. "But will you go back to the Embassy just for today? I will come for you this evening."

"The Embassy?" Atalanta faltered.

"It is only for a few hours, my precious."

"What time . . . will you come . . . for me?"

"I am not certain," Paul replied. "It might be before dinner, it might be after. Behave quite normally as if nothing had happened, but do not be alone with your cousin. He will not expect you to be anything but hurt and angry after the humiliation of being locked in your bedroom."

"Is there . . . nowhere else I can . . . stay?" Atalanta asked.

"Nowhere where I could be certain that you would be safe and that I would not be worried," Paul answered.

"Then I will go back," Atalanta said in a very small voice.

"Oh, *ma désirée!*" Paul cried. "It is a great deal to ask of you, I realise that. But at least I shall know where you are—I shall know nothing can happen until I come for you and then we will confront them together. We will tell them we are married and that you are my wife and nothing and nobody in world can separate us."

Atalanta clung to him.

"It will be a . . . very long day before I see . . . you again," she whispered.

Then she gave a little cry.

"Paul, I have just thought of something! There is a special Reception tomorrow—I mean tonight—to celebrate the Independence of Vallon. If you have not come for me before then, shall I go to it? They will expect me to do so because it is to be announced that William is the new Ambassador."

"If I cannot reach you before dinner, my love," Paul

191

replied, "go to the Reception. I will come for you there or I will meet you at the Embassy immediately afterwards."

"Suppose they prevent you from entering the building?" Atalanta inquired.

"No one will prevent me from entering any building where you are!" Paul answered.

Atalanta smiled as she thought of how he had climbed through the window and they had escaped over the roofs.

"No one would believe it possible that you would get into the Embassy unseen or that I could escape from a locked bedroom," she said.

"Then trust me," Paul pleaded. "I promise you that tonight we will tell your Aunt and your cousin that you are married to me. After that there will be nothing they can do to spoil our happiness. We shall be together and that is all I ask of life."

"And all I will ever want," Atalanta whispered.

He kissed her very gently. Then he said: "Come, my Sweetheart. If we are to go back we must hurry, otherwise the sun will be up and someone might see us clambering over the rooftops. They would think it strange to say the very least of it."

Atalanta laughed.

"I love you!" she said. "If nothing else, it is tremendous fun being married to you!"

"Which is just what I was thinking myself," Paul answered in a deep voice.

Chapter Nine

ATALANTA opened her eyes and for a moment could not realise where she was.

She had been dreaming that she was in Paul's arms and her happiness seemed to envelop her like a golden cloud.

Then, with the sunlight now seeping through the edges of the closed curtains, she saw the outlines of her room at the Embassy and remembered how she had returned with Paul over the roofs as the dawn was breaking.

He had clambered into the bedroom after her and held her closely in his arms.

"I hate to leave you, my precious love," he said. "I want, above all things, to be with you every moment, every second of the day. You know that I would not do this unless it was absolutely essential for us both."

"Yes, I know that," she said softly.

"You are tired, my sweet," he said. "Go to sleep

193

quickly and dream of me. I shall be counting the hours until we are together again."

He kissed her, a long, deep, slow kiss which seemed to draw her heart from her body, and then he had gone out through the window and she was alone.

She undressed, closed the curtains, and got into bed. Almost as her head touched the pillow, she fell asleep.

"I wanted to think! I wanted to remember!" she told herself now and knew there would be time for that during the day. With a tender smile on her face she looked towards the clock.

For a moment she thought it must have stopped and then incredulously she saw it was nearly noon.

What could have happened? Why had she been left alone? Was she still locked in?

The questions seemed to tumble over themselves in her mind and instinctively she reached towards the bell-cord. As she did so, she saw her wedding ring on her left hand.

She took it off and hid it under the pillow. Later in the day, she thought, she would put it in a piece of muslin and pin it inside her dress. Then she pulled the bell.

It was only a few seconds before the door opened and Marie appeared.

"You have had a good sleep, M'selle?" she asked.

"What has happened? Why is it so late?" Atalanta asked.

"Her Ladyship went out early and took Lady Clementine with her," Marie explained. "She gave me the key and told me that I could release you. But when I looked in, you were fast asleep."

"I never heard you," Atalanta said.

"I was like a little mouse, M'selle, because I thought you were tired," Marie explained with a smile. "So I let you sleep. There is no hurry; luncheon is at half after one today because there is a special party for the British Ambassador to Austria."

"I had better get up at once," Atalanta said. "I would like a bath please, Marie."

When she was dressed, Atalanta found to her relief that there was no chance of her having to talk with the Countess or Clementine before luncheon.

In fact they met downstairs in the *Salon Blanc et Or* where the other guests were assembling.

Atalanta had one look at Clementine's face and wondered how no one seemed to notice how unhappy and distressed she appeared.

But she thought that her Aunt, and perhaps anyone else who was interested, would suppose it was because she was nervous rather than positively miserable.

William was not present at luncheon and Atalanta tried to talk naturally with the gentlemen seated on either side of her.

It was a long, drawn-out meal and half the afternoon had gone before finally the guests retired into the garden. Lady Fitzalan's little girls came down as usual to talk to the guests and help to hand round the petits fours and chocolates.

Miss Dill looked pale and there were lines under her eyes, but otherwise she seemed composed.

Atalanta moved unobtrusively across to speak to her.

"Are you all right?" she asked softly.

"Thanks to you, Miss Lynton, I am no longer desperate," Miss Dill replied.

"Perhaps when you are at the Convent I shall be able to come and see you," Atalanta said. "I shall certainly try."

"I cannot thank you enough for everything," Miss Dill answered.

One of the Aides-de-camp claimed Atalanta's attention and there was no chance to speak further. The Ambassador was ready to make his farewells and soon the party dispersed, leaving the Countess and Clementine alone.

"You look extremely tired, Clementine," the Countess

remarked, apparently noticing her daughter's looks for the first time.

"I am all right, Mama."

"You know how important it is to look your very best tonight," the Countess said in a scolding voice. "I meant to take you to Monsieur Worth to have a final fitting for the white-lace dress you are to wear, but it seemed to me that you had better rest and get some colour back into your face. The Prince will think he has a ghost for a bride."

"I am sorry, Mama," Clementine replied in a voice which sounded as if she might break down at any moment.

"Would you like me, Aunt Louise, to come with you to Monsieur Worth?" Atalanta asked quickly to distract the Countess's attention from Clementine.

"Certainly not, Atalanta," the Countess replied. "I have no wish for your company. In fact, if you too are going to the party tonight—and I would certainly not wish William to be more ashamed of you than he is already—you, too, had better rest."

"Very well, Aunt Louise," Atalanta replied.

Her aunt looked at her closely before she said:

"If you will give me your word of honour, Atalanta, not to leave your room, then I will not lock you in. I have no wish to arouse comment in the Embassy, which will undoubtedly happen if you are treated like a prisoner."

"I should imagine it has done that already," Atalanta said with a touch of spirit.

"If it has, it is entirely your own fault," the Countess retorted. "Do you give me your word?"

"I give you my promise, Aunt Louise, that I will not leave my bedroom until I am dressed for dinner," Atalanta replied.

She felt that this was a safe promise to make because, after all, if Paul called for her she would have to be dressed before she went downstairs, and anyway he had said he would come either before dinner or afterwards.

There was no likelihood of his arriving during the afternoon.

"Very well, then," the Countess said sternly. "I trust you, Atalanta, though goodness knows I have no reason to do so. Now go and lie down, both of you. And I have told the hairdresser, Clementine, to come at six-thirty to arrange your hair. For Heaven's sake, girl, smile—this is the most important and memorable day in your life."

"Yes, Mama," Clementine murmured, and her voice broke on a sob.

The Countess looked at her in astonishment, but before she could be questioned further, Clementine turned and hurried towards the house. After a second, Atalanta followed her.

The two girls reached the second floor. Then Clementine, reaching out to take Atalanta's hands, said brokenly: "Oh, Atalanta, what can I do?"

"Can you not persuade the Duc to change his mind?" Atalanta asked.

"He wrote me a wonderful letter this morning," Clementine whispered. "He said he would love me all his life. He said there would never be anyone else, but Vallon and his loyalty to the Prince must come before everything else."

The tears ran down her cheeks as she went on.

"I respect him for it; I know he is a man of honour. But, oh, Atalanta, you cannot imagine what I am suffering!"

"I am sorry, so very, very sorry," Atalanta replied.

She turned to listen as she spoke and they both heard the Countess coming up the stairs. Clementine ran into her room for fear her Mother should see her tears.

Atalanta went to her own bedroom, took off her dress, and lay down on the bed. Despite her long sleep, she was still a little tired and she knew that it was the best thing possible for her to rest now.

She would need all her strength if she and Paul were

197

to leave Paris that evening, or must search for somewhere to stay. For they would not dare go back to the Studio.

Atalanta wondered where they would go, but it did not seem to matter. If they were together, that was Paradise enough.

She snuggled her face against the pillow and felt herself thrill as she remembered how last night Paul had murmured words of love, half in French and half in English.

He kissed her, as he had said he wished to do, from the top of her head to the soles of her feet, and they had both of them been carried away by a rapture which was beyond words, almost beyond thought.

"I love you, I love you," Atalanta whispered now as she thought of Paul, and finally she fell asleep still murmuring the words into her pillow.

Marie came to call her just before seven o'clock. She opened the door, looked round as if she thought Atalanta might not be alone, disappeared for a moment, and returned with a large box in her hand.

"What is that?" Atalanta asked.

"I think it is a present for you, M'selle."

"A present?"

Atalanta jumped out of bed and pulled on her muslin wrapper over her nightgown. Marie shut the door behind her.

"It was brought by the same man who delivered the note when you first came here," she said. "He said it was only to be given to you when there was no one else present."

"That would be Jules!" Atalanta said.

"He is a very nice man," Marie said. "I think he knew that he could trust me."

Marie put the box on the bed and Atalanta opened it. Then she gave a little gasp, for inside the box was written the name of Worth.

She pulled aside layers of tissue paper and saw,

shimmering and glittering in the box, the most wonderful gown she could ever have imagined.

She stared at it incredulously, thinking there must be some mistake, until she saw a small note and opened the envelope quickly.

It was in Paul's handwriting and she read:

For you, my Beloved, so that you will look like the moonlight which shone on us both last night. Je t'adore.

For a moment, Atalanta could almost hear Paul's voice saying the words and then as she pressed the note against her breast she stared down at the gown.

Marie helped her lift it from the box and Atalanta saw exactly why Paul had chosen it.

Beneath the white gauze of which the dress was made, there was the shimmer of silver lamé and tiny diamond dewdrops edged the frills and nestled amongst the gauze which encircled the décolletage like a cloud.

"*C'est ravissante!*" Marie exclaimed. "The most beautiful gown, M'selle, I have ever seen!"

"It is beautiful," Atalanta agreed.

At the same time, she felt horrified at the thought of what Paul must have paid for it.

How could he have found so much money? Had he beggared himself to buy her such a present?

Then she knew that with his uncanny perception he had realised, without her even telling him, that she had thought that she would never wear the elegant gowns that she had had fitted at Worth's, for which William was prepared to pay because they were to make her look worthy of her position as his wife.

Yes, Paul would have known what her feelings had been!

And, even though she had no regrets, he would have guessed that, womanlike, she had longed for him to see her looking as smart and as lovely as only the master hand of Worth could make a woman appear.

Then Atalanta thought of something else.

Paul would not wish to take her away from her relations wearing anything they had paid for, whether it was the new gowns from Worth, or even those that had once belonged to Clementine and which had been altered to fit her.

They were starting a new life together and in the future she would be entirely dependent on him and that is the way he would wish it to be. But he had spent so much on this one gown!

Atalanta could not help feeling it was wrong of him, even though she knew it had been an act of love.

Then, with a little leap of her heart, she thought of something else. That he could afford the gown must mean only one thing—that he had been successful in obtaining a commission for the murals or had sold a picture! And perhaps he had even been paid something in advance!

Her eyes lit up at the thought. She felt she wanted to cry aloud her gladness and dance for joy.

"Oh, Marie! Marie!" she exclaimed. "I am so happy!"

"I thought you must be, M'selle," Marie said. "And now hurry and have your bath and let us see how beautiful you can look in this magnificent gown."

There was no doubt when Atalanta looked in the mirror that the gown was becoming, and what was more she saw exactly what Paul meant when he said she would look like moonlight.

The shimmering silver beneath the gauze gave her an ethereal look, as if she were hardly human, but rather a spirit from the moon.

And when she and Marie lifted the gown from the box, they found there was also enclosed a tiny wreath made of petals edged with diamonds. Marie placed it on her head and arranged her golden curls beneath it.

Last night, Atalanta remembered, Paul had kissed her hair again and again.

"It is like sunshine," he said in his deep voice, "the sunshine you brought with you when you came across the park that day you walked into my heart, my darling, so that I could never be free again."

"Do you ... want to be?" she had whispered.

"Do you imagine I am not a willing captive?" he replied before his lips found hers, so she could not reply.

Atalanta turned from the mirror.

"No one has asked for me, have they?" she inquired of Marie.

"I don't think so, M'selle. If anyone had, one of the footmen would have told me you were wanted."

Atalanta decided she would not go downstairs until the very last moment.

There was always the chance that Paul would call before dinner, in which case she would want to meet him alone rather than in the Salon.

Although she knew she need not be afraid when he was with her, she could not help a tremor running through her at the imagination of William's fury and her aunt's contempt.

They would never understand that love was more important than anything else, and she knew that just as her Mother had been, she would be the object of their contemptuous compassion for the rest of her life.

They would humiliate her whenever they got the chance, they would sneer at her circumstances, and they would make it clear that they thought she was nothing but a fool.

But what did it matter? If she had to suffer on behalf of Paul, then she was glad to do so.

And perhaps it was only right, she thought, that she should suffer a little, because even in her overwhelming happiness she must not forget her family and the effect of her action on them.

Paul had promised he would find her Father another incumbency and she could only pray that it would be congenial.

Then with a tender smile Atalanta remembered that

as long as her Father could go on writing he would not really mind where he had to live.

It was only her Mother who would be worried, lest in the neighbourhood in which they found themselves there did not live people who would offer hospitality to the twins and prove agreeable to Bernard.

"Whatever happens," Atalanta told herself, "whatever lies ahead, I shall never regret for one moment that I was brave enough to marry Paul."

She could feel her wedding ring lying between her breasts in the little muslin bag which she had pinned to her bodice.

In a very short time now, she could place it on her finger and the world would know that she was Paul's wife.

Atalanta felt a quiver run through her at the thought.

His wife!

He would be beside her and she would know the strength of him, and that his eyes were looking down into hers, telling her that he loved her.

"Oh, Paul! Paul!" she whispered, and thought the time would never pass.

It was nearly eight o'clock when Atalanta went down into the *Salon Blanc et Or* where the Ambassador was receiving his guests at the dinner he was giving before the Reception at the Vallon Embassy.

Atalanta slipped unobtrusively into the room, but her Aunt saw her and stared at her in astonishment.

"Is that a dress from Madame Trevais?" she asked. "It is certainly very elaborate! I cannot imagine how she managed to produce a gown of that sort for such a cheap price. If she is as clever as that, I shall take Clementine to her and I might even order some gowns for myself."

"I am sure Madame Trevais will be very honoured, Aunt Louise," Atalanta said demurely.

Clementine, still pale-faced and miserable, did not notice her cousin's appearance, but there was no doubt Atalanta was looking attractive because the young

Aides-de-camp came up to pay her compliments and a Member of Parliament, whom she sat next to at dinner, was so fulsome with his compliments that she felt quite embarrassed.

The dinner seemed to pass more quickly than Atalanta had feared.

Soon they were all driving towards the Vallon reception, which Atalanta found to her surprise was in the Rue du Faubourg St. Honoré only a few houses away. Nevertheless, there was no question of anyone walking.

After dinner, William had arrived to greet his Mother and then to step into the carriage and sit beside Atalanta. She felt herself shiver at his proximity.

In the light of the street lamps she saw his eyes looking at her critically as if he was trying to find something wrong on which he could comment.

Finally, with almost a sneer in his voice, he said: "You look very grand this evening. I should have thought perhaps a plain white gown would have been more appropriate."

"I am surprised you do not suggest sackcloth and ashes!" Atalanta retorted.

"Atalanta!"

There was no disguising the anger in William's voice at her impertinence. Then, when he would have said more, to Atalanta's astonishment Clementine interposed.

"Oh, leave Atalanta alone, William. She looks very lovely, as you well know."

Atalanta was grateful for her cousin's championship, but at the same time she told herself it did not matter in the least what William thought or what he said.

She hated him and after tonight she need never see him again.

They reached the Vallon Embassy, stepped onto a bright-red carpet, and into a Hall which seemed to Atalanta extremely impressive.

There were flunkeys wearing the gold and scarlet of a Royal uniform, and they were led through long corridors into a Reception Room, which was already crowded with guests.

The women were all wearing jewels, the men decorations.

Beyond the Reception Room, Atalanta could see there was a large Banquet hall. The white tablecloths were ornamented with flowers, and at the front of the head table, there were two huge ornate chairs almost like thrones, heavily ornamented with gold and with red-velvet seats.

She had, however, little time to see anything, because with the Countess and Clementine she was led right up the centre of the Reception Room to where the Duc d'Abencom stood alone, receiving the guests.

Behind him was a small platform, draped behind with curtains of red and gold and surmounted by the coat of arms of Vallon.

The Duc kissed the Countess's hand, and then, as Clementine curtsied to him, Atalanta could see the pain in his eyes and she noticed his face was almost as pale and distraught as her cousin's.

"Why cannot he be brave?" Atalanta asked herself. "Why cannot he be like Paul and take her away, marry her, and not worry about anything except their love?"

She thought how lucky she was that Paul was not afraid.

William was moving stiffly at her side and she realised that he was still incensed with her, still sulking at what he considered was her ill-bred behaviour.

The Duc greeted her with a smile.

"I hope you will enjoy our ceremonies tonight, Miss Lynton."

"I am sure I shall, Your Grace," Atalanta replied, and he turned to William.

"It is a tremendous occasion for us all, Cottesford," he said. "No one knows that better than you."

"I am glad to have played my part in the restoration of your country's Independence," William said.

"We are of course most grateful to you," the Duc replied.

But there was a reservation in his voice which told Atalanta that, however genial he might appear, he did not care personally for William.

Then the people coming up behind them were received, and William somewhat fussily pushed his Mother and Clementine to the side of the low platform and took his place beside Atalanta.

"Where is the Prince?" Atalanta asked.

She was so curious that, although she did not wish to converse with William, she could not help asking the question.

"His Royal Highness will arrive when all the guests are present," William replied. "Surely you know, Atalanta, that it is correct for everyone to assemble first."

"I had no idea," Atalanta replied.

"I am quite appalled at how much you have to learn," William said nastily.

"Perhaps I am not particularly interested," Atalanta answered.

She saw the fury in his eyes.

Then, feeling it was undignified that they should quarrel in public, she turned her head away to look round the room.

Many of the men, she thought, were extremely handsome. They were taller than most Frenchmen and she remembered hearing that the citizens of Vallon were only partly of French origin, although the language they spoke was the same.

They were certainly distinctive, Atalanta thought, and many of the women were lovely.

But as she looked closer, she saw that the jewels that sparkled in their hair and round their necks were not so valuable as might have been expected, if the wearers had represented a more prosperous country.

They must all have suffered grievously during the oc-

cupation by the Germans, and later after they were
annexed by the French.

Perhaps Paul's family had been inpoverished, Atalanta
thought, and remembered how he told her that his
Mother had died of cold and starvation in the Siege of
Paris.

"I will make it up to him," she thought. "I will make
him so happy that he will realise that money is not of
the least importance to either of us."

She thought again of what he must have paid for her
gown and felt guilty.

Then she realised that the Duc was no longer receiving the guests and everyone in the room had their
heads turned towards the platform.

Through the curtains came two trumpeters wearing
elaborate Heraldic uniforms, which Atalanta guessed
must be part of the pageantry of Vallon.

They blew a fanfare and then a man resplendently
attired in a gold embroidered State uniform, and carrying a long gold-topped stick, came onto the platform.

He struck the stick twice on the ground and said in
French: "Your Highnesses, Your Excellencies, Your
Graces, My Lords, ladies and gentlemen—His Royal
Highness, Prince Alexander of Vallon!"

He stepped to one side and onto the platform came
a tall, handsome figure wearing a white uniform with
gold epaulettes and with a broad blue ribbon stretching
diagonally across his chest.

Atalanta looked at him and shut her eyes.

"It is ridiculous!" she thought.

Paul had said that when one was in love one saw the
beloved's face everywhere one looked!

She supposed, too, that the Prince looked exactly like
Paul because Paul also came from Vallon.

Everyone in the room was cheering and clapping.

Atalanta opened her eyes. It was an illusion, of
course, but there was no doubt that, although he looked
a little older and perhaps more authoriative, the Prince
seemed to have Paul's features and even his expression.

Then he said in French: "My friends, this is a memorable and a very glorious evening for us. I have, as you know, today signed the Treaty with France which gives us back our full unrestricted independence and our Royal Sovereignty."

He paused. There was tumultuous applause.

"He even speaks like Paul," Atalanta thought.

There was a note in his voice which made her quiver as Paul's voice did when he spoke to her of love.

"There will be time for speeches later this evening," the Prince went on when the applause died down, "and you know how much I want to thank you all for your loyalty, your faith, and your endurance. But now I have three things to tell you.

"The first is that I wish to announce that I have given Royal approval to a marriage between my dear cousin and loyal supporter, the Duc d'Abencom, with Lady Clementine Combe, who is here with us this evening."

Atalanta heard both the Duc and Clementine give an audible gasp of astonishment before the applause rang out and anything they said could not be heard.

She saw the Duc put out his hands to Clementine, and her face became suddenly radiant before the Prince continued.

"The second thing I have to tell you is that we have with us here tonight the man who more than anyone else is responsible for the restoration of our rights, the man who has remained our friend through all our difficulties and to whom we can never be sufficiently grateful. I refer of course to Sir Heatherington Houghton, British Ambassador to Vallon before the occupation."

There was tremendous applause. Then the Prince said: "Sir Heatherington informed me a short while ago that he wished to retire. I have, however, persuaded him that we literally cannot do without him for the next two years when we have to reconstruct our beloved country. He has therefore consented, with the full approval of the British Government, to continue as Ambassador to Vallon."

Again there was wholehearted applause, and now Atalanta, very pale with her hands clasped tightly together, felt as if she could not breathe.

It indeed was Paul who was speaking—she was convinced it was Paul—and yet how could it be?

"And lastly," the Prince went on in his deep voice, "I hope you will all wish me happiness on this day, which is undoubtedly the happiest day of my life. Not only is my country restored to me, but I have the great honour to present to you my wife—my English wife—Her Royal Highness, Princess Atalanta of Vallon."

He turned as he spoke and held out both hands to Atalanta. For a moment she could not move, and then, as he drew her onto the platform beside him, she felt as if she must faint.

"*Je t'adore*, my Goddess, my darling, my wife!" he said in a voice which only she could hear and the cheers rang out, seeming to shake the crystal chandeliers.

After that Atalanta felt as if she moved in a wonderful dream.

Paul slipped her arm through his and led her down the centre of the room between the curtsying and bowing guests toward the Banquet Hall.

Only as they reached the two thronelike chairs did Atalanta find her voice.

"Is it . . . true?" she asked in a whisper.

"I told you to trust me, my precious," he answered. "I told you I would come for you, that we would be together, and no one would be able to separate us ever again."

She could not answer him because he was looking at her and she felt as if her voice had died in her throat.

Then there was supper, speeches, and toasts until it seemed as if everyone was infected with a wild gaiety, which was like nothing Atalanta had ever seen before.

Only when she looked round did she realise that William was not present and the Countess was looking glum. The Duc and Clementine had eyes only for each other and they appeared to be enveloped in an aura of happiness.

Atalanta had no idea how long the festivities continued.

She would have thought she must be really dreaming had not the words Paul whispered to her from time to time made her quiver with joy, and the desire and passion in his eyes made her heart turn over in her breast.

Finally, Paul said, "It is time for us to leave, my Beloved."

He led Atalanta away from the cheering guests through the Banquet Hall and back through the Reception Rooms.

It was then Atalanta realised that the wives of two of Vallon's newly appointed grandees were escorting her upstairs to her bedchamber. She had a moment of panic because she was being separated from Paul, but she knew there was nothing she could do about it.

Finally they took her into a room on the first floor, where two maids were waiting. The ladies withdrew after Atalanta had thanked them in a shy voice, and then the maids undressed her.

She saw that the room was very beautiful.

There was an enormous bed surmounted by a gilt corona from which were draped turquoise-blue hangings caught up on the side of the wall by gold angels.

There was no electric light and the room was lit with candles. One of the maids carried Atalanta's dress to the wardrobe, and as the doors opened she saw several other gowns inside.

She recognised them!

They were the gowns that had been ordered for her at Worth and for which she had been fitted.

She realised that Paul must have had them collected and paid for them, so that she would have something to wear until she had time to choose others.

She was touched by his solicitude, but she was not

at this moment interested in clothes. She could only feel bewildered because Paul was not with her.

One of the maids brushed her hair and then Atalanta, wearing a soft chiffon nightgown, which she had never seen before, slipped between the pink silk sheets and lay back against a lace-edged pillowcase.

The maids bade her good night and withdrew.

Atalanta was alone in the great room with only a candelabrum, holding three candles, burning on one side of her, the others having been extinguished.

The shadows seemed dark and rather oppressive. She thought how last night they had been together in the flower-filled Studio.

She had believed that she was going to look after Paul and perhaps work for him. She had thought they would always be together day and night.

She felt her happiness drain away from her and suddenly she was apprehensive and afraid.

Even as she felt small and insignificant in the great bed, her heart heaving in her breast, the tears not far from her eyes, the door at the far end of the room opened and Paul came in.

He was wearing a long brocade robe with a high velvet collar and wide cuffs.

He stood for a moment looking at her, and then as she said nothing he crossed the room to sit down on the side of the bed facing her.

She made no gesture towards him; she only said, in a hesitating lost little voice, "Why did . . . you not . . . tell me?"

"Principally, my darling, because I wanted you to love me for myself."

"I still do not understand how you can be . . . a Prince," Atalanta said almost childishly. "I believed you were an artist—an Impressionist."

"I am an Impressionist," Paul asserted. "When the Germans occupied my country, we fought as valiantly as we could, but the odds against us were too overwhelming. My Father had sent my Mother to Paris think-

210

ing she would be safe, but she was in ill health and died during the siege."

There was pain in his voice before he continued.

"My Father and I were under arrest and when the Germans withdrew, they took with them everything of value that our country possessed. It was then we learnt that the new Republican government of France had no intention of restoring our Sovereignty."

"How terrible!" Atalanta murmured.

"This shock, on top of my Mother's death, killed my Father," Paul continued.

Atalanta put out her hand and, for the first time, touched him.

"I am . . . sorry," she whispered.

"There was nothing I could do," he said, holding her hand in his, "but persuade the best legal brains in Vallon and Great Britain to argue our case and fight for our rights. There were endless meetings until finally I realised that I personally could do very little and I decided to live a life of my own."

There was so much unhappiness in his words that Atalanta's fingers tightened on his.

"I was already an admirer of Claude Monet," he said, "and I had a certain aptitude for painting. I asked him if I could become his pupil. I worked with him first by the river at Argenteuil; later I came to Paris."

"Did you have no money?" Atalanta asked.

"Everything I had went to help those who were still in Vallon, suffering from starvation and deprived in many cases of everything they had owned. Things got better over the years, but I still did not feel, having no official duties, that I was entitled to spend money which was desperately needed by my people."

He smiled before he added: "It may surprise you, my darling, to know that one way and another I did make enough on which to live. I was not proud and I painted quite a number of portraits in a more conventional manner. They enabled me not only to pay for my own needs, but also to help some of my friends. You saw their pictures in the Studio."

He saw the expression on Atalanta's face as she thought of the Studio and went on: "It was my home for nearly ten years, and it will always have an enchanted memory for us, my precious. But so that you shall not regret it too acutely, I want to tell you that tomorrow I am taking you away alone."

"Alone?" Atalanta asked.

"No pomp, no ceremony, no Ladies-in-Waiting, no Aides-de-camp." Paul smiled. "We have a week, my dearest love, before we make our official entrance into Vallon. In that time, we can begin our honeymoon."

"Oh, Paul . . . how wonderful!"

"I have been lent a small Château on the banks of the Loire," Paul went on. "It is very small and very simple. I thought, my sweet, we would take with us Jules and, if you wished, Marie to look after us. No one else will come near us!"

"Can we . . . really do . . . that?" Atalanta asked breathlessly.

"We can and we will!" Paul exclaimed, smiling. "You shall show me how a good wife looks after an ordinary artist who will want to make love to you, *ma petite*, my precious, by the river, in the fields, under the trees, in the woods, in sunlight, moonlight, and love light! Will that bore you, my darling?"

"How could I ever be bored with you?" Atalanta asked.

Her voice trembled because the passion in Paul's words caused thrill after thrill to run through her. Then she added: "Just to be . . . beside you is exciting beyond . . . words."

"Do I really excite you?" Paul asked hoarsely.

But before she could answer he continued.

"I must not touch you until you have heard the rest of the story. Sir Heatherington, to whom I can never be sufficiently grateful, helped us win the battle against the French, but he wanted me to have an

212

English wife. There is a long tradition of English Princesses in the reigning House of Vallon. My Grandmother was English and so was my Great-grandmother."

"And your Mother?" Atalanta asked.

"My Mother was Hungarian," Paul answered.

"Perhaps that is why . . ." Atalanta started impulsively, then stopped.

"Why what?" Paul asked.

She blushed and her eyes fell before his.

"I have read that . . . Hungarians are wonderful . . . lovers," she whispered.

"You must say that to me again," he said in his deep voice. "In fact I will ask you to repeat it in a very short while, but first I must finish all that I have to say."

"Papa!" Atalanta ejaculated.

"Yes, your Papa!" Paul answered. "And your Mother, Chryseis, Hebe, and of course Bernard. I have sent one of my Aides-de-camp to England early this morning with instructions to inform your Father and Mother exactly what has happened and to tell them that you are my wife."

Atalanta drew a deep breath as she murmured, "They will be very . . . surprised."

"I also told him," Paul went on, "to ask your Father if he would honour Vallon by becoming Chancellor of our University. It is a position, Atalanta, for which my people have a great respect. I think your Father would enjoy the company of men as clever and as learned as himself and also he will have plenty of time for his writing."

"Oh, how kind you are!" Atalanta exclaimed.

"Bernard can either finish his time at Oxford or join the Army. I am sure he fancies a Cavalry regiment," Paul continued. "And later he can come and help me build up my Army in Vallon."

Atalanta gave a little cry of sheer happiness.

"And as for the twins, I think I can leave them to your Mama and yourself," Paul said with a smile. "We are a very gay country and I am related to most of the Crowned heads of Europe. I think you will be able to see that the twins are well received and have plenty of eligible suitors when it is time for them to be married. But let us hope they also, like us, find love."

"I hope so, too," Atalanta murmured.

"I wonder if you will ever know," Paul said, "what it meant to me when last night you married, as you thought, an unknown and impoverished artist?"

Atalanta did not reply and he continued.

"I expect you realise by now that I reached you, and you climbed down, through the attic in this house. Marie told me where to find your room. We were actually married in Notre Dame by my Royal Chaplain. You are joined to me, Atalanta, by God and man—there is no escape."

"Do you think . . . I would ever . . . want to leave you?" Atalanta cried.

He did not answer for a moment. Then looking at her he said, very gently, "And now shall we talk about us? Why were you feeling forlorn and looking a little sad when I came into the room?"

Atalanta gave a deep sigh.

"I was . . . thinking," she said, her voice trembling, "that it is all so . . . grand and overpowering. I wanted to look after you, to cook for you, to work for you, and now I am . . . afraid . . . afraid I shall . . . lose you."

Her voice faltered away into silence.

To her astonishment, Paul did not put his arms out toward her, but instead he rose and blew out the candles at her side.

"Oh, it is so dark!" she exclaimed involuntarily.

And then she heard the jingle of the curtain rings as he pulled back the curtains and threw open the casement.

The moonlight flooded into the room, the same moon that last night had made the Studio an enchanted place once again dazzling Atalanta's eyes with its silver mystery.

She sat staring at it and at the stars twinkling in the sable sky before she gave a little cry of surprise.

She had not realised that Paul had left the window and was in bed close beside her, drawing her into his arms.

"Have I not told you, my darling, that there is no darkness in love? Does it matter, when we are together like this, whether we are in the Studio in Montmartre, in a Palace, or anywhere else?"

His lips were close to hers and she felt his hands gently pulling the chiffon nightgown from her white shoulder.

"Do you love me?" he asked. "Do you love me enough to do all I want you to do for me in the future?"

"You know that I will do . . . anything that you ask of . . . me," Atalanta replied.

Her heart had begun to beat wildly and she felt herself quiver at the touch of his hands on her body.

"It will not be easy, my precious," Paul said. "I shall want you to sympathise with, help, and inspire so many people, and most of all I want you to love me because without your love I cannot possibly do all that there is for me to do."

He held her closer still before he said: "I went to England because I could not bear the thought of a *mariage de convenance* even though I knew it was for the good of my country. I thought vaguely that if I met the girl first we might become friends.

"I had the feeling it was somehow important for me to see Castle Combe, to get to know through less conventional channels the girl who was to be my wife."

He kissed Atalanta's forehead.

"You know what happened, my sweet," he said. "I saw a small Goddess walking across the park in the sunshine, so beautiful, so utterly alluring, that never again will it be possible for me to find another woman desirable."

He kissed Atalanta's eyes.

"I fell in love, Atalanta, and I love you as I did not

215

believe it possible to love anyone. I have given you my heart and my soul and now tell me what you feel for me."

Atalanta could feel his heart beating against hers; his hands were awakening the fire within her which she knew was burning in him.

She put her arms round his neck drawing him closer and still closer to her.

"I love . . . you," she whispered. "I love you . . . until there is . . . nothing else in the . . . world but . . . love. I will work for . . . you and do . . . anything you ask of me . . . but love me . . . because without your love I would no longer wish . . . to live."

He kissed her neck and she felt a flame streak through her body as he said hoarsely:

"I shall worship you through all eternity! You are mine, Atalanta, mine until the stars fall from the sky and the world no longer exists!"

His lips, passionate, demanding, possessive, were against hers. Then as she surrendered herself utterly and completely to his desire, she heard him murmur: "I love you, Heart of my Heart—*je t'adore.*"

ABOUT THE AUTHOR

BARBARA CARTLAND, the celebrated romantic author, historian, playwright, lecturer, political speaker and television personality, has now written 135 books. Mrs. Cartland has had a number of historical books published and several biographical ones, including that of her brother, Major Ronald Cartland, who was the first Member of Parliament to be killed in the War. This book had a preface by Sir Winston Churchill.

In private life, Barbara Cartland, who is a Commander of the Order of St. John of Jerusalem, has fought for better conditions and salaries for Midwives and Nurses. As President of the Royal College of Midwives (Hertfordshire Branch), she has been invested with the first Badge of Office ever given in Great Britain, which was subscribed to by the Midwives themselves. She has also championed the cause for old people and founded the first Romany Gypsy Camp in the world.

Mrs. Cartland is deeply interested in Vitamin Therapy and is President of the British National Association for Health.